W9-ATD-346

"I don't understand."

"Oysters, figs, pomegranate, vanilla crème?" He raised a brow. "Those are known aphrodisiacs that heighten the senses. They make you aware of everything and *everyone*."

He stopped walking and turned to her. "And I'm very well aware of you, Kimberly Parker. I've been aware of you and wanting to kiss you for some time now, so I think it's about time I did something about it."

Before Kimberly could protest or deny the very real attraction between them, Jack bent his head and his mouth feasted on hers. The shock of having his lips on hers and feeling his hard, compelling body against her was like a jolt of electricity. She couldn't help but respond by winding her arms around his neck. He took that as an invitation and took more.

His tongue dived inside her mouth and skillfully merged with hers, stroking her over and over again. His teeth incited wild thrills inside her as he nipped and teased at her mouth. Kimberly responded to his fervent ardor by grasping his head in her hands and allowing him to devour her mouth—that was the only word she could use to describe the way he ravished her. He took his time drawing out each sensation, and she delighted in his warm exploration because it matched her need.

When he finally lifted his head and their lips parted, he said, "That was just as good as I imagined it would be."

DISCARD

Dear Reader,

I'm excited to share *Heat Wave of Desire*, the first book in the California Desert Dreams trilogy, with you. Collaborating and brainstorming ideas with authors Lisa Marie Perry and Pamela Yaye was a blast.

Headstrong heroine Kimberly Parker was recently put in charge of her family's resort, Belleza, much to her brother Sean's dismay. She's drawn to mysterious, sexy guest Jack Scott. Little does she know he's the überrich son of one her top competitors. Wanna know a secret? I added a scene with Sean, hero of book three, to give readers a taste of the drama to come.

My next Kimani project is in the works! If you can't wait that long, visit yahrahstjohn.com to download my latest ebooks. Feel free to write me at yahrah@yahrahstjohn.com.

Sincerely,

Yahrah St. John

DISCARD

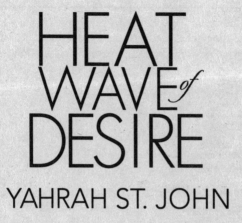

HEAT WAVE *of* DESIRE

YAHRAH ST. JOHN

⬧ **HARLEQUIN**® KIMANI™ ROMANCE

If you purchased this book without a cover you should be aware that this book is stolen property. It was reported as "unsold and destroyed" to the publisher, and neither the author nor the publisher has received any payment for this "stripped book."

Recycling programs
for this product may
not exist in your area.

ISBN-13: 978-0-373-86405-8

Heat Wave of Desire

Copyright © 2015 by Harlequin Books S.A.

All rights reserved. The reproduction, transmission or utilization of this work in whole or in part in any form by any electronic, mechanical or other means, now known or hereinafter invented, including xerography, photocopying and recording, or in any information storage or retrieval system, is forbidden without written permission. For permission please contact Harlequin Kimani, 225 Duncan Mill Road, Toronto, Ontario M3B 3K9, Canada.

This is a work of fiction. Names, characters, places and incidents are either the product of the author's imagination or are used fictitiously, and any resemblance to actual persons, living or dead, business establishments, events or locales is entirely coincidental.

® and TM are trademarks of Harlequin Enterprises Limited or its corporate affiliates. Trademarks indicated with ® are registered in the United States Patent and Trademark Office, the Canadian Intellectual Property Office and in other countries.

For questions and comments about the quality of this book please contact us at CustomerService@Harlequin.com.

HARLEQUIN®
www.Harlequin.com

Printed in U.S.A.

Yahrah St. John is the author of fourteen Kimani Romance titles. St. John is the recipient of the 2013 RT Reviewers' Choice Award for Best Kimani Romance for *A Chance with You*. A graduate of Hyde Park Career Academy, she earned a bachelor of arts degree in English from Northwestern University. St. John is a member of Romance Writers of America but is an avid reader of all genres. She enjoys the arts, cooking, traveling, basketball and adventure sports, but her true passion remains writing. St. John lives in sunny Orlando. For more information, please visit yahrahstjohn.com.

Books by Yahrah St. John

Harlequin Kimani Romance

Visit the Author Profile page at Harlequin.com for more titles.

To my creative and always resourceful sister
Kimberly Marie Mitchell for helping boost my brand.

Chapter 1

"I want it."

Kimberly Parker, general manager of the Belleza Resort and Spa, didn't wait long after her two best friends sat down to breakfast at one of the resort's three luxurious pools on Monday morning. She started in on resort business. Located in the town of Belleza, the resort was a hundred or so miles east of Los Angeles. Though it was considered a desert town, Kimberly would never tire of the breathtaking mountain views surrounding the resort's luscious grounds.

"Want what?" Robyn Henderson asked. As the event planner for the resort, she managed special events for their private guests and corporate clients.

Gabrielle Royce, the executive chef, looked equally confused. "I'm with Robyn on this one. What is it you want?" She glanced longingly at the sumptuous egg-white veggie soufflé she'd prepared for their breakfast, which they hadn't yet touched. But Kimberly had business not breakfast on her mind.

"I want the Dunham Foundation gala," she explained, reaching for the glass of orange juice Jessica, their waitress, had placed on the table for her. She didn't have to ask because Jessica knew the ladies' morning ritual. They always sat down to a health-conscious breakfast after an intense workout and Pilates at the Belleza's three-thousand-square-foot gym.

Kimberly had changed into her usual attire for the day—a lavender silk shirt, cream pantsuit and pumps—and had pulled her hair back in a sleek ponytail. Robyn had donned a simple black pencil skirt with an orange cap-sleeved shirt and low sling-back heels. While Gabrielle opted for distressed jeans and a graphic T-shirt under her chef coat and her ubiquitous PUMAs. They each had such different styles, but they'd been thick as thieves for years.

Robyn was the tallest of the bunch, with creamy tapioca skin and hazel eyes. She wore her hair in a sophisticated updo. Gabrielle was short, five foot three to be exact, and had a mass of unruly auburn curls and brown eyes. She had a fairer complexion than Robyn's, while Kimberly was the odd man out with her broad nose, almond-shaped brown eyes and dark caramel skin.

"Ah." Robyn nodded her head in understanding. "I'd heard the illustrious Dunham family was in the market for a venue for their annual gala, but I didn't know the Belleza was in the running."

Kimberly nodded. "Not that I wish anyone ill, but the Beverly Wilshire, where they normally hold the Dunham gala, had a major flood a week ago. The damage was so extensive that the remediation and repairs will take months. Their misfortune is our gain. Which is why we can't let it slip through our fingers." She practically rubbed her hands together in glee.

"And we won't," Gabrielle responded. "The Dunhams aren't our first high-profile client. We've had scads of celebrities come here in recent years. Isn't that R & B singer Cole on-site now?" She patted Kimberly's arm. "Don't worry. We've got this, Kim."

Gabrielle was right. The resort had hosted innumerable big-time guests. Surely the Dunhams would be just as satisfied. And she remembered that though her friend didn't know them personally, Gabrielle's parents had been acquainted with the Dunhams for years.

She smiled at her friends whom she'd known since meeting them at the Merriweather Academy boarding school when she was fourteen. She didn't know why she was letting this event get her worked up. Hadn't she been the one to help her parents oversee the renovation that had revitalized the resort? Now people were flocking from all over the world to stay at the Belleza. But all her success had come at a price. She'd lost both her brothers in the process.

"Kim!"

"Hmm?" Kimberly blinked, bringing herself back to the conversation. "What was that?" She turned to Robyn.

"I asked you when the Dunhams are coming."

"Hayley Dunham is coming at the end of the week and we need to be prepared."

"That isn't much notice," Gabrielle stated.

"True," Kimberly replied, "but this golden goose has just come to roost and we can't pass up this opportunity."

"And you want to go all out for a consult, I presume?" Robyn inquired.

"Of course," Kimberly stated. "We can give them a preview of what we can do from the music, the flowers, the food, the ambience. Show them there's no place better than the Belleza."

"You don't have to convince me," Robyn responded. "Or Gabby for that matter. We've drunk the Belleza Kool-Aid and absolutely love this place. Whatever we can do to convince the Dunhams," she said as she pointed her nose upward, "that we are worthy of them, we'll do."

"Fabulous." Kimberly beamed at them. "I knew you wouldn't let me down."

"The Dunhams aren't the only clients to express interest in holding an event at Belleza," Robyn replied. She pulled a manila folder out of her oversize Louis Vuitton tote and opened it.

Robyn updated them on other potential event prospects, but Kimberly's attention was momentarily distracted when she saw extended-stay guest Jack Scott sit across from them. The quiet, handsome guest had been at the Belleza for the past three weeks. It was somewhat unusual for a guest to stay so long, especially when it didn't appear that he was conducting any business. Then again she'd often seen his head buried in a tablet.

"I have some great ideas about changes to the spring menu that I'm sure your prospect might enjoy," Gabrielle enthused. "I'm thinking of doing a chilled corn soup with bacon jam, and a seared scallop and braised pork belly with a polenta cake. And for dessert—" she paused for effect "—a lemon vanilla crème with mint puree and hazelnut sable crumbles."

"That sounds delicious, Gabby." Robyn licked her lips in anticipation. "Doesn't it, Kim?"

"Oh, yes," Kimberly replied, turning her gaze back to her friends. "Those are all wonderful selections and we'll need it to compete against The Pinnacle." Several travel magazines had already done features on the new resort opening up about thirty minutes away.

"Do you really think we'll have some competition?" Gabrielle inquired. "The Belleza has been a staple in this community for years."

"Which is why we can't rest on our laurels," Kimberly pointed out. "We have to keep up with the ever-changing market. We don't want to appear boring or old or stale.

We want to be fresh, innovative and cutting-edge. We must constantly reinvent the resort."

"That's exactly how I describe the Belleza to corporate clients," Robyn added.

"Good," Kimberly said. "With our long-standing reputation for class and quality, we have a step up over The Pinnacle, which is just a start-up. But they will be looking at ways to eat up the market share, so we have to be diligent in our efforts. I think all three of us should present during your corporate client consults, Robyn. Show them why the Belleza is a step above the rest."

"Agreed," Robyn said. "I'll send everyone invites. But if you don't mind, I'd like to eat my soufflé before it gets cold."

"Dig in." But instead of looking down at her breakfast, Kimberly's eyes darted across the pool and connected with Jack Scott's dark brown ones.

He'd been caught staring.

Jaxon Dunham had been watching the three women from across the pool as they ate, laughed and talked. It was pretty hard not to stare when they'd had the same routine each morning since nearly three weeks ago when he'd first caught sight of *her*. He'd been unable to stop himself from coming down here to watch them.

The one who'd caught his eye was about five foot seven inches tall, had caramel-colored skin and long silky black hair. Despite the pantsuit she was wearing, which he'd seen in a variety of different colors over the past three weeks, it was evident she was shapely and toned underneath. But what sparked his interest even more was the confident aura with which she carried herself.

He suspected she was in a position of power given the way she disseminated orders to the staff around her, but it wasn't in a harsh way. From where he was sitting, he could see she treated her employees fairly and with respect. It went a long way in his book. The problem was he wasn't supposed to be looking at *any* woman. He'd come to Belleza for a vacation from his family and had sworn off women, all because of Stephanie Sawyer.

He'd been casually dating Stephanie for the past few months because he'd been trying to stop his parents from pushing him toward the altar. His parents expected Jaxon to do as they'd done. When he'd reached thirty, his father, Charles Dunham, had agreed to an arranged marriage with Claire Butler, who was of his same class. Since Jaxon was now thirty-two years old, his parents wanted him to do the same. *Stephanie's from a good family*, his mother had said, *and you need to settle down and start a family.*

So at his mother's constant urging, Jaxon had finally agreed to start seeing Stephanie. From the outset, he'd explained to Stephanie that he had no intention of marrying, but he'd thought if they dated, his family would get off his back. He'd thought Stephanie had been cool with the no-strings-attached arrangement. At least until two months ago.

Over dinner with both the Dunham and Sawyer families present, his mother had announced their engagement. Jaxon had been furious and he'd thought Stephanie had been, too. He'd been wrong. The next morning, when their engagement was announced in the society pages, Jaxon had gone to Stephanie's place to figure out damage control. And that was when he discovered that Stephanie was in on the whole thing.

"Getting married is a great idea," she'd said. "Haven't I shown you how good we can be together?"

When he'd disagreed, she'd attempted to entice him

into the engagement by getting him into bed. When that didn't work, she'd threatened to sully his reputation in the media. Stephanie knew how important the Dunham family image was. They'd been a long-standing family in the Beverly Hills community for half a century and he wasn't about to let her ruin that. Jaxon had pointed out that blackmail was no way to begin a partnership and he wouldn't let *her*, his family or anyone force him into marriage. When he was ready, he'd choose his own wife. He wouldn't have an arranged marriage like his parents. Instead, it would be one of mutual love, passion and respect. Stephanie had vowed revenge, but he hadn't cared.

Furious with his parents for getting him into this debacle, he'd packed his bags and left the family estate in Beverly Hills. At first, he'd thought about leaving the country, but then had thought better of it. Why not hide in plain sight? He'd been hearing great things about the Belleza from research his family had done for an upcoming gala, so he'd decided to give it a try.

He'd been at the Belleza for the past three weeks under a false name. Everyone at the resort believed him to be Jack Scott. They had no idea he was really Jaxon Dunham, member of the über rich and powerful Dunham family of Beverly Hills. He was glad they didn't, because they treated him like a regular person instead of someone born to privilege.

Even though he was wealthy and considered by some to be born with a silver spoon in his mouth, Jaxon didn't shirk his duties to the family business. The Dunhams had made the bulk of their money in financial investing through Dunham Investments, and forty-five years ago, his grandparents had formed the Dunham Foundation to help those less fortunate.

Finance was Jaxon's specialty at Dunham Investments

and the Foundation, which coincidentally allowed him the chance to work remotely instead of having to work on-site at the corporate offices in Beverly Hills. He could conduct business from his laptop or iPad and lay low with no one being the wiser. Until the brunette!

Thinking about how those cream-colored pants hugged the caramel beauty's toned behind stopped Jaxon from focusing on his iPad and the society page of the *Beverly Hills Times*. Stephanie had been airing their dirty laundry to whomever she could get to listen to her rants. Couldn't they see *she* was a jilted woman? No, they wanted to sell newspapers and the Dunham name made for good fodder. He could easily sling the hash back at Stephanie, but what would that accomplish except fuel the flame?

He would stay here at the Belleza until the dust settled. But something told him he wouldn't be alone for long.

Kimberly tried focusing on the girls' conversation, but her mind kept wandering back to Jack Scott. There was something about the mysterious stranger that was appealing.

She looked in his direction again and once more her gaze collided with his and she quickly looked away. She hadn't expected to be caught checking him out again.

"Looks like someone's got it bad," Robyn teased.

"Who?" Her eyes grew large with wonder.

"You." Robyn laughed. "I saw the way you were looking at Jack Scott like you wanted to sop him up with a biscuit."

"Robyn!"

"You're talking about the superhot guy who checked in a few weeks ago, but has been primarily keeping to himself?" Gabrielle asked.

"The very same," Robyn said. "And Kim here has been unable to stop staring at him since we sat down."

"That's not true." But her denial sounded weak.

"Is too," Robyn countered.

"A girl can look, right? Given our no-dating-guests policy, there's nothing to worry about." Kimberly attempted to act as if she was unaffected by the handsome and mysterious guest. The truth was, he was by far the most attractive man she'd seen in ages. In her position as general manager, she rarely had time to date, if at all.

"Are you sure about that?" Robyn asked. "Because you're not the only one doing the admiring."

"What do you mean?" Kimberly was afraid to hazard another glance in Jack's direction for fear he would find her out.

"He's not looking at me or Gabby," Robyn responded. "He hasn't been able to take his eyes off *you*."

A flurry of butterflies swarmed in Kimberly's belly. He *had* been looking at her. She hadn't imagined it.

Kimberly cocked her head to one side. "Well, he can look all he wants, but you know I don't fraternize with the clientele."

"I agree. The rules are in place for a reason," Gabrielle said. "They prevent us from being put in a bad spot."

"I don't know, Gabby," Robyn replied. "If any rule was made to be broken, it would be for a date with that fine specimen of a man."

"You needn't worry," Kimberly replied, "because I will not be breaking that rule. The policy is in place to preserve our reputation and I'm not just talking about the resort. People come on vacation looking for a fling and I won't be another notch on the bedpost."

"It's too bad he's a guest," Gabrielle said, "because

maybe it might loosen you up some." She patted Kimberly's arm. "When was the last time you got laid?"

"Gabby, you're incorrigible!"

"But she also hit the nail on the head. When was the last time?" Robyn pressed.

Kimberly didn't answer. Couldn't. It had been a long time since she'd had a date, let alone got intimate with a man. She'd been so focused on reinventing the Belleza to the exclusion of all else that her love life had dwindled to next to nothing. Ben Lawson was the last man she'd dated and her friends knew that hadn't ended well.

Ben had accused her of being a workaholic and too self-involved to put someone else, him in particular, first. His words had hurt, but his departure from her life hadn't. Kimberly hadn't been shattered by his disappearance. In fact, she'd just worked harder, striving for success to prove to her brothers and the Belleza staff that her parents had made the right decision in putting her at the helm of the resort. But in the back of her mind, Kimberly had always wondered. Could Ben be right? Was she too selfish to consider someone else's needs above her own?

"You should go talk to him," Robyn urged.

"I don't know…" Gabrielle said.

Kimberly thought about sex as much as the next woman and she enjoyed male company. She refused to end up a spinster or alone like Jonah Grady. As much as she loved the elderly bartender who'd been at the Belleza since its early humble beginnings, she didn't want to be alone as she went into maturity, so she made a split decision and rose.

"All right, all right," Kimberly said once on her feet. "If it'll get you two hens off my back, I'll go talk to him." She gave them both a wink and started toward Jack Scott.

Chapter 2

I can't believe I'm doing this, Kimberly thought as she made her way across the to Jack's table. Perhaps if she got the curiosity out of her system, she could go back to business as usual.

Jack Scott was sitting under an umbrella with a plate of fruit, toast and a cup of black coffee. He looked up as she approached and his brow quirked, but that didn't stop his eyes from roaming over every inch of her.

She offered a smile. "Good morning."

"Good morning."

God, why does his voice sound like hot maple syrup over buttermilk pancakes?

Finding her voice, she said, "I haven't had the opportunity to introduce myself. I'm Kimberly Parker, general manager of the Belleza. Please allow me to welcome you to the resort. I understand you've been staying with us for several weeks. Are you having a pleasant stay?"

Why did she have to sound so trite? Did he sense her uneasiness? It was out of character for her to make the first move, let alone talk to a male guest outside of business, but there was something about him that intrigued her.

He smiled back at her. "My stay has been very enjoyable. Your staff has a way of making the Belleza feel like my home away from home."

"That's the promise we deliver on," Kimberly replied. "Can I offer you a complimentary mimosa or Bloody Mary?"

"Thank you, but I prefer to keep a clear head. Maybe another time?" His face split into a wide grin.

That was the opening and she'd hoped to smoothly transition into her manager routine.

"I—" All words escaped Kimberly at his disarming smile.

Jack motioned to the seat across from him. "Care to join me?"

"I, uh—" Her mind went blank and she couldn't think of a single thing to say. Instead, she merely nodded. Before she could make a move, Jack Scott jumped up and pulled a chair out for her. She walked over and took a seat. "Thank you." She finally found her voice.

"The pleasure is mine," he said.

Kim offered a genuine smile.

"I've seen you around the resort," he replied. "But you're always running around and appear quite busy."

She shrugged. "It isn't easy managing a resort of this size alone."

He frowned. "I'd heard the Belleza was a family business. Am I mistaken?"

Kimberly shook her head. "No, you're not. It's just that…" Her voice trailed off.

"Just that what?"

"I shouldn't talk about it here." She looked around the pool area, but only a handful of people were milling around. A few were at the breakfast buffet and several others were swimming in the pool. Meanwhile Robyn and Gabby were blatantly staring at them from across the way.

"Seems like you have a lot on your mind," Jack replied. "Sometimes it helps to talk about it."

He was very intuitive, Kimberly realized, if he could pick up on her duress mere minutes after meeting her. Was it written all over her face? "I guess I do."

"Care to tell me?"

"It's nothing really," she replied, avoiding his piercing gaze.

"Why don't you let me be the judge of that?"

Kimberly laughed at his bossiness. "All right, if you must know, not everyone in my family is as happy as I am that I've been named general manager of the Belleza. You would think they'd approve, given all the time and effort I've put into the renovations. After all I've given—" She stopped herself before she revealed too much.

"Are they jealous?"

Kimberly frowned. "Perhaps, but I don't believe that's the only reason."

"What else could there be?"

"My older brother felt like it was his birthright and that I stole the job from him. Sean and other staff members assumed because he was the oldest, he was an automatic shoo-in for the position. But if I was just in it for myself, why did I suggest to my parents that Sean and I run the Belleza together?"

"Hmm…" Jack nodded in understanding.

"What?"

He shrugged. "Well, from Sean's position he didn't want a consolation prize, and if I were him, I'd have to agree. If my parents didn't deem me worthy of the responsibility I wouldn't want any of it."

"So you're taking his side?"

He shook his head. "Not at all. I'm just trying to get

you to see things from his side and that the situation isn't black-and-white."

"I get what you're saying and I know it was a tough pill for Sean to swallow, but if the shoe were on the other foot, I would have supported him no matter what. I'd be proud of him."

"Then you're a better woman than most," Jack responded, "considering it would have squashed your own dreams."

"But that's what you do for family."

"I agree with you, but he's too hurt to see that now. Give him time. I'm sure he'll come around."

"I hope so. We've always been so close and I hate having this division between me and my big brother." Kimberly couldn't help the tears that stung her eyes. But she didn't want to blubber in front of this handsome man.

Jack reached across the table and laid his large hand on hers. "It's okay. Disagreements happen in families, but if the love is there, in time you'll get over the hurt and disappointment. And who knows, your relationship might be better for it in the end."

Kimberly stared at Jack. If anyone had told her that this sexy stranger would be so insightful, she would have told them they were a liar, but he was. And he'd made her feel as if there was hope for her and Sean's relationship. "Thank you. What do I owe you for the session?"

He laughed. "You owe me nothing. Well, perhaps—"

He didn't finish his sentence because Kimberly's cell phone rang on her hip. "Sorry. I have to take this." She rose from the table, stepped several paces away and took the call.

When she returned several minutes later, she apologized. "I'm sorry, but I have some important business to attend to."

"Not a problem," Jack replied. "I'm sure I'll be seeing you around."

Kimberly nodded and began walking away. She sure hoped she'd be seeing a lot of Jack Scott around.

After she'd gone, Jaxon exhaled deeply. Kimberly Parker was even more beautiful up close. She'd been more approachable than he'd ever seen her, and a bit vulnerable. He hadn't expected her to confide in him of her family and business troubles, but he was glad she had because he could relate. He knew what it was like to be angry with your family and to want to write off the lot of them. Not that he would. He just needed time to cool off.

Staying at the Belleza was supposed to be a retreat, a time to reassess his life and come up with a game plan, not fall for the first beautiful lady that came into his view. But Kimberly Parker wasn't just another set of legs. She had brains and wit. How else could she have achieved the success she had at the Belleza? But what surprised him the most was that she was more than just a suit hiding behind her work. She had heart.

The way she'd talked about taking a backseat if her brother had been chosen to run the resort told Jaxon just how special she truly was. And that was trouble. He wasn't just attracted to her physically, even though the sparks had been flying back and forth between them during their exchange. No, he was also attracted to her spirit. And that was much worse.

If he intended to keep his vow of not getting involved with another woman, he'd have to keep his distance.

Yes, Kimberly Parker was a big problem.

* * *

After she finished handling a small inventory crisis with cleaning and bedroom supplies, Kimberly returned to the administration offices to study labor and revenue reports to get a sense of yesterday's results. Then she began forecasting the day ahead, studying any issues that might arise. Some VIPs were due to arrive at the hotel that afternoon, and a significant catering event was coming up this weekend.

Still, her mind wandered to the short time she'd spent with Jack Scott earlier. He'd been an excellent conversationalist and she'd felt comfortable opening up to him, which had surprised the heck out of her. She hadn't intended to be so honest about her family with Jack, yet—and that was when it hit her. During the entire conversation, Jack hadn't revealed a single thing about himself.

Robyn poked her head into Kimberly's office.

"C'mon in." She motioned her forward.

"So," Robyn asked, her eyes wide and full of questions, "how did it go with Jack Scott?"

"Couldn't you tell?" Kimberly asked. "You guys were gawking."

"We were not." Robyn lowered her head. "Anyway, someone had to give you a little push."

"He was a perfect gentleman," Kimberly replied. "And kind."

"Kind?" Robyn said. "That wouldn't have been the word I would have used to describe him from where we were sitting. Hot. Sexy. Gorgeous. Fine. Those are all words I would use."

Kimberly chuckled. "And normally I would agree if Jack hadn't shown me that he's more than a pretty face."

"How so?"

"Somehow I ended up pouring out my heart to him about Sean."

"Sean?" Kimberly noticed that Robyn's ears perked up at the mention of Sean's name. At times, she'd wondered if Robyn fancied her brother, because she was always popping up in his kitchen, but nothing had ever come of it, so Kimberly had dismissed the notion. "What about him?"

"I told him that Sean was angry that he wasn't chosen to run the Belleza." Kimberly rose and walked to the windows. She stared out. The administration offices overlooked the Plaza's lush foliage with palm trees and man-made bridges and ponds. "I still can't believe he just quit and cut all ties with the family, Robyn." She turned to look back at her friend. "And Jack... Well, he could see that I'm still struggling with the loss and offered—"

"Comfort and a warm bed?" Robyn interjected, trying to lighten the mood and make her laugh.

And Kimberly did laugh. Something she hadn't done enough of lately. "He offered me some words of wisdom."

"Sounds promising."

"Doesn't matter." She walked back over to her desk and slid into her executive chair. "Because it won't happen again."

"Why not?"

"You know my policy on dating guests."

"Policies are made to be broken," Robyn said, sitting on Kimberly's desk. "Jack Scott got you to open up about a subject you've been pretty closemouthed about the last few months, even to me and Gabby. There's something there. Don't you owe it to yourself to find out? What harm would be there to share a meal with the man?"

"Perhaps." That was all Kimberly was willing to concede.

As if sensing she couldn't keep pushing Kim or she'd

bolt in the opposite direction, Robyn changed the subject. "So, have you heard from Sean?"

Kimberly shook her head. "Nope. And it sucks. I miss him."

"I heard he's opening up his own restaurant in LA. The SP Grill."

"I—I heard those rumors, too," Kimberly replied, "And I wish him much success. Really I do. But we could have run this place together, like Batman and Robin. No pun intended."

Robyn laughed. "Maybe you will one day. In the meantime, I'd like to go over the Brooks wedding for Saturday night."

"Let's get to it."

Kimberly was busy for the remainder of the afternoon, walking around the hotel, visiting with staff, answering emails or having lunch with a congressman's aide to prepare for his arrival. She finished the day by holding her daily staff meeting before the shift change. At 6:00 p.m., she was finally able to leave the resort to go to the Parker family home because she had some paperwork her parents needed to sign. After the promotion, she'd been so busy she hadn't had a chance to visit them much. Or so she told herself. Deep down, she knew that wasn't the only reason she hadn't gone home.

Family dinners felt empty without her two brothers, Sean and Ryan. Sean had left and gone to Los Angeles, while her younger brother, Ryan, had taken his guitar and headed for New York. He'd said it was to strike out on his own and finally make a go of his music career. Even though she knew Ryan's interest extended beyond the resort, Kimberly knew the real reason he'd gone at just that moment: he'd sided with Sean and had abandoned her, too.

She swiped her access card against the panel, and the large wrought-iron gates opened, allowing her entry into the Parker compound. Her parents lived in a large Spanish Colonial–style house just a few miles from the Belleza Resort and Spa. The two-story main house had white stucco walls and a red-tiled roof. There were also a pool house and a two-bedroom guesthouse on the grounds.

As she got out of her red Audi S7, Kimberly looked up at the wrought-iron balcony facing the large swimming pool. She'd spent many a summer there just reading a good book while Sean and Ryan played in the pool below her. Her head had always been in a book back then. She smiled at the fond memory as she walked up the cobblestoned path of the long driveway up to the house.

She heard music coming from the side of the house and walked up the side path to find her mother in a big straw hat and apron tending to her garden. Ilene Parker was proud she'd been able to maintain a vegetable and herb garden given the desert climate around them. She was knee-deep in dirt without any gloves on. Why did her mother persist in not taking care of herself? Kimberly resolved to get her a pair.

Her mother must have sensed her presence because she turned around. "Kimberly!" The happiness in her mother's voice made Kimberly feel bad for keeping her distance.

"Mom." She bent down to give her mother a hug while lending her a hand to rise to her feet. Her mother looked comfortable in her jean capris, T-shirt and tennis shoes.

"Not that I'm not happy to see you, but what are you doing here?" her mother asked, wiping her hands on her apron. "I didn't prepare anything special for supper, just some homemade chicken soup and salad. I came down here to get some fresh tomatoes."

"It's okay, Mom," Kimberly responded. "I just came by to get you and Dad to sign some final paperwork about the management turnover. I'm not really hungry."

"Okay. We can take care of that over dinner."

As usual her mother didn't listen and insisted that she stay for supper.

"Where's Daddy?" She looked up at the stucco house.

"In front of the television watching the Golf Channel."

Kimberly laughed. Her father had always been an avid golf watcher, but now that he'd retired he was enjoying playing the sport, as well.

"I should go inside and have him sign these."

"They can wait," her mother said, removing her big straw hat. Her reddish-brown hair had been pulled back in a bun. "Why don't you tell me how it's going at the Belleza. How are you coping with all the changes?"

"Well, I'm honored at the faith you and Daddy have in me."

"But…"

"But nothing. I can do the job. No, correction. I was born to do the job. Sean was always in the kitchen creating masterpieces, while I," she asserted, as she patted her chest, "worked all over the hotel, absorbing as much information as I could from you, from Daddy, from anyone and everyone. I developed the marketing plan that put the Belleza back on the map and reminded folks of our history, not to mention those pesky rumors of a buried treasure stashed on the property."

Her mother smiled at the reference. "You certainly capitalized on that with your 'Discover a world of hidden riches' theme when you renamed the common areas after precious gems. That campaign was ingenious, baby girl. Emerald Empire, Sapphire Sanctuary, Ruby Retreat and of course The Pearl were featured in luxury travel magazines because of you."

Kimberly smiled. "Thank you, Mama. That's why I can say without any doubt that I *earned* my place."

"Earned what?" her father said from the top of the deck that overlooked her mother's garden.

"Earned a right to come over for dinner unannounced," Kimberly replied, glancing in her mother's direction. She knew her father didn't want to rehash this topic. He'd made his decision and didn't appreciate it being second-guessed.

"Of course," her father said. "You don't need to ask. This is your home. Whatcha got in your hands?"

He inclined his head toward the manila envelope she held.

"Some papers for you to sign."

"Well, come on up," he said, "and let's take care of the business before your mama finishes up supper."

Kimberly touched her mother's shoulder as a sign that they would talk later. Once Kurt Parker made an edict, they all followed. She climbed the concrete steps from the garden up to the deck at the back of the house and found her father sitting in one of the wicker rockers outside.

"Daddy." She came forward and bent down to give him a hug. "How's retirement treating you?"

He pushed up his silver-rimmed glasses. "I'm still adjusting," he said gruffly. "Miss the resort, but I'll make do."

"We miss you, too."

Her father guffawed. "No, you don't. You're like me. I know you're glad to have the run of the place without my interference."

Kimberly shrugged. "I guess the apple doesn't fall too far from the tree?" She smiled at him. His face didn't look a day over fifty, she thought, though his salt-and-pepper hair and mustache gave away his age. For some reason she felt a little sentimental looking at him. Perhaps her conversation with Jack had made her a touch homesick.

"Never has," her father said. "But all is well?"

She shook off her thoughts. "Yes, everything is fine."

"You know you don't fool me," her father replied. "You've always been a bad liar, Kimberly. So why don't you tell me what's really going on?"

"Can't I visit my parents without the Spanish Inquisition?" She rose in a huff from her seat.

"Sit back down, girl."

Kimberly rolled her eyes at the commanding tone in his voice. Once upon a time, it would have stricken her with fear, but not anymore. But out of respect, she walked back to her seat.

"This is about your brother?"

Kimberly nodded and was irked that he could read her so easily. "Have you heard? Sean's opening a new restaurant."

"Not from him." Her father reached for a cigar out of his cigar box next to the rocker. He cut the edge with a guillotine and lit it up. "One of my pals at the club told me while we were out on the ninth hole. Imagine my surprise to hear this from a stranger and not from your brother."

"I had no idea, either, until Robyn told me today," Kimberly responded. "I tried to play it off like I knew, but I didn't. I mean I know he always wanted a place to call his own."

"He had that at The Pearl."

"Apparently he didn't think so. For him, being executive chef at The Pearl and managing the resort went hand in hand. He didn't want one without the other."

"Your brother is stubborn," he said as he puffed on his cigar. "He couldn't see what I see."

"Which is?"

"The big picture. He internalized my decision, when it was strictly business. There's a lot more to the Belleza than just the kitchen, as you're fully aware."

"I am."

"Then good, let's not beat the dead horse. I wish your brother much success with his newest endeavor, but I don't regret my decision for one moment."

Just then, her mother came up the steps with a wicker basket full of large, plump tomatoes. "How about some dinner?"

Kimberly breathed a long sigh of relief. Coming here had been the right choice. Hearing her father reaffirm his decision that she run the Belleza was exactly what she needed to hear. "Thanks, Daddy."

Chapter 3

"Have you seen the papers?" Jaxon's best friend, Nate Griffin, asked him on the phone the following morning as Jaxon walked into the Belleza's gym for his morning workout.

"No, what are they saying now?" Jaxon stopped short of the doors and stepped aside for some privacy. He didn't want anyone hearing his conversation or associating him with the Dunham family.

"Stephanie is claiming that you made promises to her, that you went back on your word."

"You know I never promised that woman a darn thing," Jaxon responded harshly. "We agreed to a mutually beneficial dating scenario, which once over should have been over."

"She doesn't seem to think so. She's telling every gossip columnist or blogger in the Beverly Hills area that you broke her heart and she's completely devastated."

"Well, if she's looking for sympathy, she's not going to get any from me," Jaxon replied. "Did I tell you she's the one who told my parents we were getting engaged?"

"No, you didn't. You just rushed off and left Beverly Hills without a word."

"I'm sorry about that, but I had to bounce. The heat was on."

"Where are you?"

"Can't tell you that," Jaxon said. Walls had ears and he didn't want anyone in his family to find out where he was until he was good and ready.

"I'm supposed to be your boy."

"And you still are. I just need some time away from the Dunham clan—hell, from the entire situation. To get some perspective. You understand?"

"Of course I do. I have your back. I could have told you that Stephanie was no good. Those society types are always looking for a husband. When she saw you, she saw fresh meat."

Jaxon laughed at the analogy. "I'll talk to you soon, Nate. I gotta get my workout on."

"All right, Jaxon, take care of yourself, man."

"You can bank on it."

Jaxon ended the call and pulled the handle to enter the facility. The Parker family had spared no expense when they'd renovated the Belleza a few years ago. The gym was state-of-the-art. It had the usual equipment and flat screens, but it also contained a glass-fronted fridge with cold water, towels, alcohol wipes and, most important, a killer view of the mountains. He was about to head over to the rows of free weights when a curvy backside caught his attention. He would know that backside anywhere. It was the same one that had him up last night wondering what it would be like to run his hands over it.

It didn't help that she was wearing one of those skimpy outfits that women loved to wear to the gym under the guise of working out. Most wanted to show off their figures and have men take notice. Kimberly, however, appeared oblivious to the appreciative stares of the men in the gym. The hot-pink halter sports bra and matching capris she wore looked as if she'd been spray-painted into them. They revealed her sculpted arms, legs and firm behind.

He walked over to the treadmill where Kimberly was jogging and added a taut stomach to that description of her amazing figure. It was well earned because even though she was running at a steady pace, only a light sheen was on her forehead. She had on earbuds, so he was forced to move in front of the treadmill to catch her eye. When he did, she stumbled and had to press Stop on the treadmill to prevent herself from falling.

"Are you okay?" he inquired, rushing over to her side.

"I'm fine," she said with annoyance. "Or I would have been if you hadn't startled me."

"I merely walked in front of your machine. I imagine I wasn't the first this morning." His gaze swept across the gym, which was half-full with guests. "By the way, good morning, Kimberly."

She smiled and Jaxon's heart instantly melted. She needed to smile more often instead of wearing her usual stern expression. "Good morning, Jack."

He liked hearing his nickname on her lips. It was too bad he couldn't tell her who he really was.

"Want some company?" He eyed the empty treadmill beside her.

She glanced to her side. "Only if you can keep up."

A broad grin spread across Jaxon's face. "Is that a dare? Because I warn you I used to run track in college."

"And how long ago was that?" she asked, laughing as she restarted her treadmill to a slow walk.

"You're on." Jaxon eyes blazed laughter as he stepped up onto the treadmill beside her.

Kimberly bunched her shoulders. "It's your funeral."

Jaxon wasn't above a challenge. In fact, he welcomed it and began increasing the speed on his treadmill to match her fast walking pace. "How often do you come to the gym?"

"Five days a week," Kimberly replied. "Sometimes seven if I can make it, but five is the minimum."

"You're very disciplined. Not many people make working out a daily habit."

"It gets results," she said, "plus, it allows me to pretty much eat whatever I want. In moderation, of course."

"That's the key, right? Most people miss the moderation part."

"You don't look like you're one of them." The moment the uncensored comment came out of her mouth, she instantly looked down to adjust her treadmill.

So she had noticed his physique? Jaxon was glad he wasn't the only one feeling the chemistry between them. It had been just as strong as the day before when they'd talked after breakfast. And now, sexual tension crackled between them.

"Like you, I try to maintain," Jaxon replied. "My regimen is two days cardio, three days weight training. Works for me."

Kimberly shot him a furtive glance out the corner of her eye. He could see she was trying her best not to check him out in his tank top and shorts, but she was. And from the looks of it, she liked what she saw.

"So, are we going to do this or what?" she inquired. "I typically go three miles and I'd just got started when you interrupted me."

"Then you'll get a little bit extra in today," Jaxon responded. "Let's go." He quickly increased the speed on his treadmill and took off running.

Kimberly caught up to his pace and joined him in the quest for domination of the treadmill. She kept up with him for the first mile and a half, but after that Kimberly slowed.

"Ready to give up?" he asked at the second mile.

"Hell no."

He laughed at her passionate response. Kimberly had a feisty side to her and he liked it. He liked it a lot.

"I don't give up," she added. "So I'll finish. Even if I'm last, I'll finish."

In the end, he finished several minutes ahead of her, but he had to give the woman props on her fortitude. She kept pressing on until she completed the three miles.

When she stopped and jumped off the treadmill, she was no longer misty as before, but had a fine sheen of perspiration on her face and running down the valley between her breasts, which he couldn't help but notice. "You won." She held out her hand. "Fair and square."

He grasped her hand in his. "And what do I win?" He held it for a long time and their eyes connected. A quick burst of desire made him want to pull her into his arms, kiss her senseless, remove the sweat-drenched clothing from her body and make her sweat underneath him.

"I…" Words seemed to escape her and he liked that he had her off balance.

He just had to have a taste of her. He was about to act on his impulse, without a thought that they weren't alone, when a feminine voice yelled, "Kim!"

Hearing her name broke the trance and she blinked several times and released his hand. "Thanks for the run." She inclined her head toward him and started in the direction of the voice.

He watched her saunter over to her friends. They talked in hushed tones and one of them—the one with the auburn curls—glanced in his direction, before her arm was quickly wrenched away.

Damn! He'd been so close to paradise. If only he hadn't been interrupted. What was wrong with him? He felt like a hormone-raging teenage boy without any self-control. He had to get ahold of himself. He'd told himself no romantic entanglements. But at the first sight of a hot body, he was ready to forget about his promise. But if anyone could make him want to forget his edict, it would be Kimberly Parker.

Oh, Lord! Kimberly fanned her face as she approached Gabrielle and Robyn. Why had she agreed to Jack's challenge when she'd sworn she'd stay away from him? Her policy was no interaction with the guests, but Jack Scott had her breaking all the rules.

"Hey, Kim." Gabrielle eyed her up and down. "Looks like you got a head start on us this morning." Her head inclined in Jack's direction.

"Oh that." Kimberly laughed, but even to her ears it sounded shaky. "That was nothing. Just a little challenge among friends."

"Are you sure about that?" Robyn inquired. "Because when we walked in, you two were holding hands."

"We—we weren't holding hands," Kimberly responded. "We were *shaking* hands after he won our bet and beat me jogging."

"Is that right?" Gabrielle sounded skeptical as she headed for the mats. Kimberly and Robyn followed her. Gabrielle wasted no time, dropping to the mat to begin her morning stretch routine and Robyn did the same.

"It is," Kimberly said with her hands on her hips as she looked down at them. "There's nothing going on between us."

"Tell that to the choir," Robyn said. "Because we know

you, Kim, and sexual heat was coming off you in waves—
still is."

Kimberly turned back around to glance at Jack, who'd
moved from free weights to the bench press. He'd found
a partner to assist him as he lifted the dumbbell up and
down. Even from her vantage point, she could see the
definition of his muscles.

"Earth to Kim." Gabrielle snapped her fingers.

Kimberly spun around. "What?"

Gabrielle shook her head and shrugged as she stretched
her torso to the right. "Nothing."

"I have to get a move on it this morning, so I'll see
you both later at the staff meeting." She made her way
toward the gym's exit.

"No breakfast?" Robyn inquired.

"Can't. I have a conference call." Seconds later, Kimberly was out of the room. She didn't want her friends to
catch on to just how attracted she was to Jack because she
didn't understand it herself. Could she keep him at arm's
length? Or was it just a matter of time before she gave in?

Chapter 4

Kimberly took a quick shower at her condo at the resort before making her way to the office to go over some paperwork. Gabby and Robyn each had their own condo in the same building. A decade ago, her father had erected the luxurious condominiums in the rear of the resort behind the villas and hotel buildings so that staff and timeshare members could enjoy the Belleza lifestyle. It was an added bonus for Kimberly because she was close by if needed.

With work so close to home, Kimberly knew she was considered a workaholic, but she enjoyed the day-to-day running of a resort this size and didn't consider it mundane. With a bachelor of science in Hospitality Management from California State University in Long Beach and her ten years' experience working full-time summers and part-time during the school year, she was more than capable of handling the Belleza's complex operations.

Speaking of, she had a laundry list of items on her agenda for today. She took care of the immediate fires, did her daily walkabout and completed one of her quality assurance checks for the month before stepping into the staff meeting later that afternoon.

Among the others already present were Robyn and Gabrielle, as well as Allison Haines, the Rooms division manager, Megan Johnson, the director of Food and Beverage, and Kimberly's assistant manager, Antoine Colbert.

"Good afternoon, everyone." Kimberly took a seat at the head of the table.

There were several rumbles before Kimberly got down to business. After taking care of the usual business, she made it to her favorite topic: special events and the tasting menu.

"The Belleza is in the running for the annual Dunham Foundation gala in a couple of months," Kimberly began. "Due to a flood at the Beverly Wilshire, they have to make a change and try someplace new."

"That's fantastic," Megan replied.

"Yes, which is why our presentation to Hayley Dunham needs to be the best we've ever done. The recognition of having the Dunhams here and the potential referrals would really solidify our position as *the* venue for special events."

"When are they coming?" Robyn inquired. "I have some preliminary mock-ups that I've begun sketching out this morning that we can go over."

"That's great," Kimberly said, "but we also need Gabrielle's hand all over this." She glanced at her best friend. "We have to show them you're the best executive chef on the West Coast."

"Even though Sean is gone?" one of the other staff members responded with a snort. "Everyone came to the Belleza because of his reputation."

"Yeah," another staffer joined in. "Did you hear he's opening up his own restaurant?"

There were several whispers among the crowd.

"Settle down." Kimberly glared at the man who started the conversation; she could see out of the corner of her eye that Gabrielle had been mortally offended by his comment. Kimberly suspected some of the staff had doubts about the kitchen living up to its reputation since her brother had left. But Gabrielle was a skilled chef and Kimberly would not let her be disrespected. "Sean was talented, no doubt, but Gabrielle is our secret weapon. The Belleza will shine with Gabrielle at the helm."

She smiled at the chef, who offered a fake smile. She knew her friend well enough to know that the comments had struck a nerve. "Gabrielle, why don't you tell us what's on tap for this month's tasting menu?"

The experience was open to only a few select guests who were considered to be the crème de la crème. Gabrielle had designed some creative selections for their sophisticated palates. Now Kimberly was forcing her to face her fears and not let the staff comments get her down.

Gabrielle cleared her throat before speaking. She started off slowly with her initial comments about her starter, but bounced back with a livelier description of her second course, entrée and dessert. By the end, she had everyone at the meeting salivating.

After the meeting ended, her employees began filtering out. Gabrielle tried to make a fast getaway, but Kimberly called out to her. "Can you stay behind for a moment?"

Robyn stayed behind, too, and when it was just the three of them, Kimberly closed the door.

"Kim, do we have to do this now?" Gabrielle asked sharply. Now that the door was closed, all pretense of confidence had gone away.

"Yes, we do."

"Why can't you let this rest?"

"When has she ever let anything rest?" Robyn replied. "You know how she gets."

"I can't let you go when you're upset, not without talking about it first."

"Why talk? It won't change anything." Gabrielle's tone was chilly as she continued, "All those people think I got my job as executive chef out of nepotism. That because you and I are friends, I was chosen to step into the role."

"But it's not true," Robyn said firmly. "You're a damn good chef, Gabby."

"I know that!" Gabrielle blurted out. "But they don't. And I won't change their opinion anytime soon. I'll have to earn their respect day by day and I'm fine with that. Do you think this is my first rodeo? It's not. Do you think it was easy turning my back on medical school and choosing the culinary field? Do you think it was easy when I came back to the States after France and dealt with the old boys' network in New York? Well, it wasn't."

"Of course," Kimberly said. She knew how hard it had been for Gabrielle to go against her parents' wishes. Even more so when they'd cut off her trust fund. Thank God for her grandmother's financial support. It had allowed Gabby to attend culinary school in France, otherwise who knew how long it would have taken for Gabby to realize her dream. "I didn't mean to imply otherwise." She patted her chest and inclined her head to Robyn. "We know that it wasn't an easy road for you, but you have persevered and all I wanted to say is that I have your back."

"That's all?"

Kimberly nodded. "That's it in a nutshell. I wouldn't have appointed you and my father wouldn't have backed me if we didn't think you *were* and *are* the chef to keep the Belleza at the top."

"Thank you, Kim. That means a lot. I guess I just needed to hear it."

Kimberly patted her hand. "We all do sometimes."

Yesterday, she'd needed the very same thing from her father. "So how about we all look at the mock-ups that Robyn prepared to wow Hayley Dunham and talk menus?"

Over the next hour, she, Robyn and Gabrielle did just that. By the end they'd agreed to present three themes to Hayley Dunham, who was coming in two days. It would give Gabrielle enough time to purchase several items that were critical to the complicated four-course menu that included a dessert using molecular gastronomy.

"Are you sure you haven't put too much on yourself?" Kimberly asked her. "It's an elaborate one."

"It is, but it'll guarantee us winning the Dunham contract," Gabrielle replied. "And it's important to me that we do."

"You don't have to prove anything to anyone," Robyn said. "If anything goes wrong…"

"Nothing will go wrong." Gabrielle popped up from her chair. "This would be a big coup for us. I can just see my parents' faces now…" Her voice trailed as she stared out the window.

"What about them?" Kimberly asked.

"They've attended the Dunham gala every year," Gabrielle answered.

"Did you?" Robyn asked.

Kimberly knew Robyn had grown up in the projects. Her friend looked a bit starstruck at the thought of Gabrielle at such a lavish event.

Gabrielle shook her head. "No, it wasn't really my thing, but my parents always did. Can you imagine how shocked they would be to learn that I am partially behind its success?"

"It would certainly make a statement," Robyn replied.

"Then it's no-holds-barred," Kimberly said. "We go

all out." Gabrielle wasn't the only one with something to prove. She would show her parents and her brothers that she could make the Belleza an even greater success. There was no doubt in her mind that with her and her friends' hard work, it would be.

Instead of going to the pool, which was his usual MO for this time of day, Jaxon stayed in his villa. He wasn't going to be present in Beverly Hills for the Dunham Foundation Board of Directors' meeting, but he would call in. Despite how angry he was with his parents, the work he did at the Dunham Foundation was important to him and he wouldn't shirk it.

How could he when it was founded by his great-grandparents? They'd given a twenty-five-thousand-dollar donation to start the Foundation during a time of great unrest in the country. African-Americans were fighting against injustice and his grandparents had wanted to help those less fortunate during those tough times. The Foundation had come a long way from its humble beginnings.

Today, the Dunham Foundation was a success because they'd harnessed his grandparents' initial investments into future growth capital, which was part of the work Jaxon oversaw among his other duties as director. In addition to promoting democratic values and reducing injustice, the Foundation gave grants to reduce poverty, foster cultural expression, strengthen children's futures with higher education and deepen connections to nature and community around them.

He dialed the Foundation's number and Pam, the receptionist, answered.

"Jaxon," she whispered into the phone. "Your parents are fit to be tied that you didn't return for the meeting."

"I expected as much, but thanks for the heads-up, Pam. Patch me through to the conference room."

"Sure thing. Good luck."

Several seconds later, the connection was made and a feminine voice asked, "Jaxon, is that you?" He didn't need to be present to know who it was. It was his mother.

"Yes, ma'am. I'm here."

"The question is why you aren't *here*?" his father asked through the line.

"Let's not get into that right now," Jaxon responded. "I assume everyone is present. Has roll call been taken?"

"No, we were just about to do it," his sister, Hayley, replied. She was secretary as well as a director at the Foundation along with his parents, his uncle, Robert, and aunt, Eleanor, and their two sons, Andre and Mason.

"Then let's get started," his father replied.

After roll call was taken, his cousin, who was in charge of grants, went through several grantee applications, highlighting their strengths and weaknesses.

"Well, I, for one, think we should finally get involved with autism," Jaxon heard his aunt Eleanor say. "The disorder is becoming more prevalent. This would be a great cause to champion."

"So are the other candidates," his father commented. "We have to look at our mission statement and see how they fit with our core values."

"I agree with Daddy, Auntie," Hayley said. "As much as that's a great cause, the local food bank Second Harvest is in desperate need of our support. I think we should consider them for the grant."

"Why can't we do both?" Jaxon asked from the other end of the line. "It doesn't have to be one over the other." He knew his sister was active in local charities, and wanted to support her.

The conversation raged on for nearly an hour with no decision before his father as president and presiding officer agreed to table the discussion to the next board meeting.

Jaxon was about to hang up when the meeting concluded but his father stopped him. "Stay on the line, son."

Jaxon was not looking forward to this discussion, but he would listen out of respect for his father. He heard voices dissipating before he said, "Yes?"

"You have your poor mother up in arms."

"She should be," Jaxon said. "She and Stephanie concocted this whole ruse to get me down the aisle and it backfired."

"You know we just want what's best for you, son."

"Let's be real, Dad. You want the next Dunham heir to carry on the family name. But I'm not there yet and you can't force my hand. Help Mom realize that, because until you do, I'm not coming home."

Abruptly, Jaxon ended the call. There wasn't anything left to be said. The only thing he wanted right now was a massage. His family had gotten him all stressed-out when he'd been in such a good place.

He picked up the receiver and quickly arranged for a relaxation massage in ten minutes. The spa had a cancellation and was able to squeeze him in. A massage would be exactly what he needed to let go of the family drama. Tearing off his T-shirt, he changed into some shorts, slipped on his flip-flops and headed out the door.

The massage was peaceful and serene and as he closed his eyes and the masseur's hands roamed over his shoulders, he let the worries of the day fade. His parents had no idea where he was, so he was free to do as he pleased. Speaking of doing as he pleased… An image of Kimberly popped into his subconscious. Her smooth caramel-colored skin, those long shapely legs that met a curvaceous bottom had him suppressing a groan.

He didn't want the masseur to think him a pervert, but the woman had invaded his thoughts when he was supposed to be relaxing. Now, instead of feeling relaxed after the massage, he felt more anxious than before. He needed to get back to his room and take a cold shower. Maybe then he could get those sexy images of Kimberly out of his mind.

He was so deep in thought as he rushed back to the villa that he didn't watch his step and collided with a warm body. His hands instinctively reached out to stop them both from falling. When he did, he felt soft and very supple curves. He glanced down and right into Kimberly's rich brown eyes.

Chapter 5

"We meet again."

Kimberly's breath caught in her chest but unlike when she saw Jack at the gym, this time he was shirtless. Her hands were now splayed across his expansive chest as she'd used him for support to keep from falling. It allowed her to see what his shirts had hidden from her view. Broad shoulders, a smattering of hair on a well-defined chest, six-pack abs... Or would it be eight-pack abs if his shorts dipped lower?

She swallowed.

"Kimberly?"

"Hmm..." She glanced up at him and wished she hadn't because she saw something in his eyes. Desire. She felt it, too. Had been feeling it since their breakfast encounter a couple of days ago. Fate, it seemed, kept putting them in each other's path.

Jack's hands roamed upward from around her waist where he'd lightly planted them to stabilize her. They threaded through her long black hair, which she'd decided on a whim to wear down rather than in her usual sensible, professional bun. He brought her forward into closer contact with his body even though Kimberly couldn't see how it was possible since they'd collided with each other in a mass of arms and bodies.

She could feel the heat emanating from his chest as she went closer, and then her nipples brushed against him, causing them to pucker underneath her silk shirt. Jack leaned down and pressed his forehead against hers and breathed her in. Kimberly tried to wiggle away, embarrassed by her traitorous body's response to him. It wasn't right that he could make her feel this way when she barely knew him.

"Don't fight it," he whispered softly.

He was lowering his mouth to hers when a loud crash sounded behind her. Jack instantly spun around, pushing Kimberly behind him.

It was a protective move that Kimberly admired, but it was hardly necessary. The noise was courtesy of Charlene Vincent, the newest hire at The Pearl, who'd just dropped a handful of menus. The girl seemed prone to mishaps.

"Sorry," the buxom blonde said, picking up the menus before rushing off in her stilettos.

"Can she even walk in those?" Jack murmured aloud.

"Clearly not." Kimberly pushed away from him and took several steps backward to give herself some distance to breathe, to think.

A smile ruffled his mouth. "What's wrong? I don't bite."

Kimberly sensed the sexual magnetism that made him so self-confident. "Are you sure about that? Because this—" she pointed between the two of them "—is not going to happen. I don't date guests."

"We aren't dating," Jack responded. "We were, however, about to kiss, which if we hadn't been interrupted would have been overdue. I know you felt it."

"Felt what?"

He raised a quirky brow. "The pull. Between you and me."

"Th-there's no pull. We just..." Kimberly couldn't think of a single, plausible reason why she'd ended up in his arms just now. He was right. If they hadn't been interrupted, they would have no doubt ended their collision with a hot, searing kiss. Her panties were nearly moist just from touching him. The prolonged anticipation was unbearable.

"Kimberly." Hearing her name on his lips was like a sensual caress washing over her. "You can't deny what's happening between us."

"I can. And I will."

"Why should you have to?" He quirked a brow. "We are two adults who are interested in each other. What's the harm in that?"

"I don't want to complicate our relationship. I'm in charge of running this hotel and—"

"And you don't want to let your parents down by taking your eye off the ball?"

How could he know what she was thinking? Feeling? He seemed to know without her verbalizing it. She'd met many attractive men before, but none like him. He wasn't vain; he was observant, kind and it made him dangerous to her well-being.

"Don't try to change the subject. I don't fraternize with guests, especially those I know nothing about."

She noticed he paused, so she had definitely given him something to chew on.

"True, you don't know much about me, but that would change if you agreed to spend some time with me."

Kimberly glanced down at her watch. "I have to go."

"All right, Kimberly Parker, but this isn't over between us."

Kimberly sure hoped it was as she stalked away back to her office. She hoped that Jack would be checking out soon and then things would go back to normal. But when she checked Jack's reservation, it was open-ended. She had no idea how long he would stay on at the Belleza. And the longer he stayed, the harder it would be to stay away from him. She was afraid her resolve might weaken and she might give in to temptation. And that was exactly what Jack was, all six feet of him.

A couple of days later, after a three-mile jog and a quick smoothie, Kimberly returned to her condo and dressed carefully for the day's big event, the Dunham presentation. She'd managed to successfully avoid any further run-ins with Jack Scott because she'd been swamped with hotel business, but it was a matter of time before their paths crossed again.

She took one of the golf carts parked near her condo and rushed toward the Plaza. Located next to the main hotel building, the Plaza housed ballrooms of various sizes, several restaurants and boutique shops for their guests. When she arrived at the Grand Ballroom, Robyn was running around arranging the decor from the floral arrangements to the linens to the crystal chandeliers they'd ordered for the event.

Kimberly grabbed Robyn's arm as she rushed past. "I thought I would come lend a hand. What can I do?"

"I have it under control."

Kimberly glanced around at the upheaval surrounding her and raised an eyebrow.

"Kim, the event isn't until 1:00 p.m. and it's only…" she said, glancing down at her watch. "Nine. We have plenty of time to arrange the tables and the decor according to the vision I created in the presentation."

"You can never have too much help," Kimberly replied. "And remember how important this presentation is for us."

"I'm well aware."

Kimberly sensed Robyn's annoyance with her constant questioning. At times it was hard to separate their friendship from work, but she wouldn't be doing her job if she didn't stay on top of her staff. "Where's Gabby?"

"In the kitchen with the pastry chef," Robyn answered as she rifled through a box. "They're putting the finishing touches on the miniature dessert display."

"Excellent, so what can I do?" Even though she was general manager, Kimberly wasn't above getting her hands dirty if things needed to get done. To her, that was the sign of a good manager.

"Well, if you must do something," Robyn said with an exasperated sigh, "why don't you get started with the display of gift boxes I've created for the registration desk outside."

"No problem." Kim walked into the hall to the large table they had set up outside. There was an array of gift boxes and various giveaways. She took off her jacket, draped it over the back of one of the chairs and dug in.

She was knee-deep in stuffing the gift boxes with chocolates and one-of-a-kind charm bracelets from their on-site jeweler that she didn't see Jack approach until he was standing right in front of her. Her pulse suddenly leaped with excitement. There was no denying the spark of attraction toward him. She was trying her best to ignore it, but it was hard not to be excited when the man was obviously interested in her. She hadn't had the time or inclination for male company in a long time. So if she was honest with herself, it was nice to be wanted.

Jack was dressed casually in white linen trousers and a matching shirt, which highlighted his coffee-colored skin.

"What are you doing here?" she blurted out. Shouldn't he be relaxing by the pool at this early hour? Why was he at the Plaza?

"Good morning to you, too."

"I'm sorry." She'd completely forgotten her manners. "Good morning. But the question is still on the table."

"Is the ballroom off-limits?" Jack inquired. "Because I thought guests were welcome throughout the hotel grounds."

Well, he'd just put her in her place. "I'm sorry." How was she apologizing again in the span of a few seconds? "You're right, of course. It's just that we— I mean I don't see guests in the ballroom foyer unless they're part of the event."

"And do you have an event coming up?"

She nodded. "This area will be closed off for a private event this afternoon."

"Sounds exciting. Who's it for? Or can't you tell?"

Kimberly glanced around. It couldn't hurt to share her excitement with Jack. It wasn't as if he was involved in any way with the Dunham Foundation. "We have a presentation with a representative from the Dunham Foundation."

"You do?" He glanced down the hall in each direction. "Are they here now?"

"Oh, no." Kimberly shook her head. "Do you think I would be this calm right now with all there is to do?" She inclined her head to the mess of gift boxes and miscellaneous items on the table.

He appeared to breathe a sigh of relief before he said, "I guess not. Do you need any help?"

Before she could say no, Jack was already coming behind the table to sit next to her. "So what are we doing here?" he asked as he surveyed the assortment of items.

"We're putting candy and jewelry in each gift box. Then we're wrapping it up in a bow, like this." She demonstrated one box to him. "But you really don't have to do this."

"I know I don't *have* to, but I want to, so just accept that you have my company until it's over."

He didn't know what he was asking of her or how hard it would be to sit beside him and act as if she was unaffected. He smelled woodsy and earthy and she just could breathe him in all day long. Instead she continued packing the goody boxes.

"Are you familiar with the Dunham Foundation?" she asked, trying to get her mind off him and on to other neutral topics.

He turned to her sharply. "Why do you ask?"

"Oh, it just sounded like you were familiar with them."

"I've heard of them." He reached for a box and began stuffing.

"So you're from the Los Angeles area?" Kim inquired.

"Roundabout."

He sure wasn't offering much information about himself. Was that what was attractive about him, the air of mystery surrounding him? "You've been at the Belleza for some time, but if you live nearby, why the long stay?"

He stopped stuffing boxes long enough to glance her way and smile. "Have I worn out my welcome?"

"Of course not. I love paying customers."

"And is that all I am to you, Kimberly? A paying customer? You don't strike me as someone afraid of taking chances. Please tell me you have the courage to admit there's something between us?"

"Between us?" she asked with a slight edge to her voice.

He stared at her long and hard and her mouth became

dry. He was calling her out, forcing her to confront what was happening between them like she'd done to Gabby. He wasn't backing down and she was finding it harder and harder to resist him. Yes, he was a guest and although they had a strict policy of no fraternization, she couldn't fight it anymore.

"I can't deny there's something between us," she finally admitted aloud to herself and to him.

"Progress."

He gave her a sideways glance as he returned to his task and closed the box.

She laughed and watched in surprise as he managed to tie a decent bow.

"What are we going to do about it?" He slid the finished product toward her on the table.

Should I go for it?

Her mind told her to stay away from him and play by the rules, but her body, her heart, told her to go for it and she did. "On Friday night we're having our monthly tasting menu. You should come to the dinner. My best friend Gabrielle goes all out. It's the highlight of her month, except perhaps today's event because she really wants to impress the Dunhams."

"I've no doubt you all will," Jack said. "Because I'm sure you succeed at everything you do."

"I certainly try."

Jaxon watched Kimberly from the ballroom doorway as she moved around the room. He could see she was champing at the bit to take charge, but she'd told him outside that her friend Robyn was the event coordinator for the hotel and in charge of pulling all the trades together from the kitchen to the event staff.

Eventually she came back to him at the door. "Robyn

has everything under control here," she said. "So I think I'll go to the kitchen and check in on Gabrielle and then head to the main lobby so I'm prepared when Hayley Dunham comes."

Jaxon swallowed. His little sister was coming to the Belleza? Great. He had to get out of Dodge quick. He didn't need Hayley to find his hiding place. Even though he knew she would keep his secret, he wanted his privacy.

"Well, I'll head out, then," Jaxon said. "I'll see you this weekend?"

"It's a date."

They shared a smile. "Good luck." As he walked away, Jaxon was happy that he'd made inroads with Kimberly. Although that hadn't been his intention when he'd come to the Belleza, he'd been unable to deny the physical connection between them. Perhaps if he just scratched the itch, it would go away. Taking Kimberly Parker to bed and unleashing the tigress he was sure was hiding beneath that perfect exterior would be fun. Unfortunately, an affair was all he could offer. He just hoped that would be enough.

Hayley Dunham was as put together as Kimberly imagined she would be. She was tall and leggy in a designer sheath and killer peep-toe alligator pumps, and perfectly coiffed in a layered bob. She arrived on time and full of vivacity. She toured the grounds with Kimberly on the golf cart, pausing at times to take in the ambience of the Belleza.

"The property is really quite spectacular," Hayley commented as Kimberly stopped the cart in front of the Plaza. "We've heard great things about the Belleza for years, but my mother had been reluctant to make a change. The flood at the Beverly Wilshire forced her to rethink the gala and think modern and exciting."

"The Belleza is all those things and more," Kimberly said as they exited the golf cart and walked through the Plaza. "We can offer your guests accommodations if they desire while the gala is held here. I know some will be traveling a couple of hours and may not want to drink and drive." She motioned upward to the Plaza. "Our Grand Ballroom can easily fit five hundred guests."

When they arrived at the ballroom, Kimberly paused in front of the double doors. "Rather than just show you the space or some presentation boards, we decided to show you the event."

"Let's have a look," Hayley said.

As she opened the door and walked in with her prospective client, Kimberly was ecstatic. Robyn hadn't disappointed. She'd created the romantic yet classically chic event she'd presented during the staff meeting. Waves of silk hung from the ceiling as did crystal chandeliers. Each table was cloaked with champagne linen and housed the finest china and crystal champagne flutes Robyn could find.

"Oh, my God!"

Kimberly beamed from ear to ear as she watched Hayley's reaction when she walked into the room.

"You did all of this for me?" Hayley asked, turning to her.

Robyn came forward to meet them. "We wanted to show you that here at the Belleza, nothing is impossible." She offered her hand. "I'm Robyn Henderson, event planner here at the Belleza."

Hayley's eyes were wide with excitement as she looked around at the table, dance floor and bars that had been set up for the event. "Did you do all this?" she asked, shaking Robyn's hand.

Robyn's face broke into a wide, open smile. "I wish I could take all the credit, but it took an army."

"But it was Robyn's vision," Kimberly stated. "One which I fully support. Wait until you sample the tasting menu our executive chef, Gabrielle Royce, has prepared for you." Kimberly motioned Hayley toward the dance floor, where a center table had been set up like the others. It would be where they would dine for lunch.

By the end of the four-course tasting lunch, Hayley Dunham was *oohing* and *aahing* over the chef and Kimberly knew they'd sealed the deal.

"Can I meet the chef who created this delicious meal?" Hayley wiped both sides of her mouth with a napkin.

"Absolutely," Kimberly said. "She's coming this way."

Hayley rose from her seat as Gabrielle came forward on the dance floor.

She'd removed her chef hat, but was proudly wearing her chef's coat, trousers and plain black mules. "I'm Gabrielle, the executive chef here at the Belleza."

"Your food is amazing," Hayley gushed, offering her hand. "I enjoyed every bite of it. I can't say this officially until I speak with the board, but take my word for it. I can't see having the Dunham Foundation gala anywhere else."

"Thank you." Gabrielle pumped her hand. "Thank you. It was a labor of love and you can be assured that my staff and I will work diligently to ensure a successful event."

"If the Belleza can go through all this for a presentation, I've no doubt you will."

Afterward Kimberly drove Hayley back to the lobby

on the golf cart and waited with her as the valet brought around her car.

"You'll be hearing from me..." Hayley's voice trailed off as she glanced in the direction of the lobby.

"Is everything okay?" Kimberly inquired, looking in the same direction.

"Oh, yes, everything is fine. I just thought I saw someone I knew." Hayley blinked several times before turning to Kimberly. "You'll be hearing from me by next week. Thank you again. You and the Belleza team know how to impress."

After Hayley had gone, Kimberly couldn't resist stomping her feet in glee. They'd done it! They'd gotten the Dunham gala and now there was no stopping them.

Just then, she noticed Jack standing in the shadows by the lobby. Had he been watching their interaction this entire time? Why didn't he come over? She would have introduced him to Hayley Dunham. It was just one of the mysteries about Jack that intrigued her and cautioned her to be careful with her heart. After all, how much did she really know about him?

Chapter 6

Kimberly was overthinking it and second-guessing the evening. Should she have invited Jack to the Belleza monthly tasting menu dinner? She tried to tell herself that he was just another guest, but she knew it wasn't true. Robyn and Gabby may think he was another of the crème de la crème of the Belleza's guests that were already on the list for evening, but he wasn't. He was her *date*. Reluctantly he'd agreed to meet her at The Pearl because she'd told him she wanted to keep their relationship private and if they came together it would raise too many eyebrows.

Since tonight was an unofficial date with Jack, Kimberly was struggling with what to wear for the evening. She'd nixed several dresses, which were now sitting in a heap on her bed. She was in a strapless bra and panties debating between a knee-length jacquard sheath and a one-shoulder white maxi dress with a side slit when she heard a knock on the door. Robyn and Gabrielle entered her condo. They both looked elegant yet sophisticated. Robyn was wearing a bright blue pleated jersey dress and wore her hair up with several tendrils down each side of her face. Gabrielle, meanwhile, had let her unruly curls free, which went perfectly with her halter jumpsuit, trio of gold necklaces and stilettos.

"You're not dressed," Gabrielle commented.

"I can't decide."

"It's not like you to be indecisive," Robyn said intuitively. "What gives?"

"Nothing," Kimberly responded but her voice sounded high even to her.

"Perhaps she's nervous because Jack Scott is coming to the tasting dinner." Robyn's mouth curved into a smile.

"Is he?" Gabrielle turned to glare at Kimberly.

"Yes, but it's not what you think," Kimberly answered in a rush of words.

"What are we thinking?" Gabrielle inquired.

"I invited him because he's one of our high-profile guests. That's all, nothing more."

"You must think we just fell off the turnip truck," Robyn said, "because I'm not buying that for a minute."

"Believe it!" Kimberly said. "Now help me pick out a dress." She held up the two options.

"If you want to have the classy-general-manager image, I would go with the sheath," Robyn stated.

"I'm going on record as stating that I am not on board with this," Gabrielle said. "But if you want to make Jack's eyes go back in his head and have his mouth hanging open, I would go with the one-shoulder maxi dress with the side slit to the thigh."

Kimberly chose the one-shoulder maxi dress. It was sexy and the slit wasn't indecent. She wore her hair bone-straight with simple gold hoops, but she added a splash with her makeup: a smoky eye, mascara and a glossy lip.

"Looking hot!" Robyn said when she'd zipped Kimberly up and she'd twirled around to look at herself in the pedestal mirror.

"We have to go," Gabrielle said. "I need to check in on the kitchen and make sure the chef is on point."

"I can't believe you're going to let go of the kitchen tonight."

"I have to enjoy life, too, plus if I can't trust them with what I've taught them, then I'm not much of an executive chef, am I?"

"You have a point," Kimberly said.

Ten minutes later, the three of them walked through the doors of The Pearl.

"Good evening," Charlene greeted them with a smile and bright red lipstick to go with her pale skin and blond hair.

"Hello, Charlene," Kimberly responded.

"Follow me." Charlene walked them to the wine room where the tasting menu was served each month, but before she could get there, the poor girl stumbled in her heels and nearly fell into a nearby table.

"I'm so sorry," Charlene said as she got to her feet.

"Are you okay?" Robyn inquired, offering her a hand.

"Yes, these are new shoes and I'm still getting used to wearing them."

"Perhaps you shouldn't wear them," Gabrielle said under her breath.

Kimberly glanced over at Gabrielle, who shook her head in annoyance.

When Kimberly walked through the wine room's glass doors and saw Jack standing there in a tailored suit, she turned to her friends. "It's a date," she whispered.

Jack was devastatingly handsome and her insides jangled with excitement. Plus, he looked as if he'd just gotten a haircut because his hair was cropped shorter than it had been earlier.

"I knew it!" Robyn snapped her fingers.

Jaxon's eyes roamed over Kimberly, starting with the shoes. She'd chosen to wear strappy sandals rather than her usual low pumps. Then there were the legs that were on display for all to see. The one-shoulder dress she wore wasn't vulgar. It wasn't low-cut or see-through, but it showed him enough expanse of leg that he didn't know how he would sit next to her tonight and *not* touch her.

And her hair was straight and silky. He suspected she'd chosen to wear it down for him and he liked it. Finally, there was her face. She didn't need the makeup, but it did enhance her features. Kimberly Parker was a beautiful woman, no doubt about it. He'd told himself he would avoid romantic entanglements while he was at the Belleza, but Kimberly made him rethink that vow. Hell, he threw that idea out the window entirely! There was a simmering, smoldering heat inside that nice, neat package and it excited Jaxon. He wanted her in his bed, on the floor, standing up, anywhere he could get her. It was just a matter of when.

He strolled over to where she stood with her friends. "Good evening, ladies."

"Mr. Scott." Robyn offered her hand.

"Call me Jack." He shook the proffered hand.

"Hello, Jack," Gabrielle said, "I'm Gabrielle, but you can call me Gabby. Everybody does."

He grasped one of Gabrielle's hands. "Pleasure to meet you." He kissed her hand, but didn't take his eyes off Kimberly.

"Well, we're going to go mingle." Robyn smiled knowingly but Jaxon didn't hear her. His eyes were on one woman.

Robyn and Gabrielle departed, leaving him alone with Kimberly. "Hi."

He could tell she was nervous because she was shifting from foot to foot.

"You look stunning tonight."

She smiled and touched the pendant necklace hanging from her neck. "Thank you."

"Your friends seem to know something," he said. He leaned over to whisper in her ear and caught a tantalizing whiff of perfume that was a mix of berries and vanilla and a hint of something else he couldn't name. "I thought we were keeping this *date* a secret."

She smiled. "We were, but I can't keep anything from them. They figured me out."

"Good, because I was going to have a hard time not ogling you in that dress tonight." He grasped her arm and led her over to the other diners: a senator, an A-list movie star, the head of a major financial corporation and Cole, the recording star. "Can I get you a drink?" He certainly needed something to cool him off. Because he would like to find the nearest utility closet, push Kimberly into it and lift that dress up and have his way with her.

"I'd love one."

Kimberly followed Jack over to the bar that had been set up in the private room. Jonah Grady was manning the bar tonight. Jonah was in his eighties, but that didn't stop him from working a few days and special events like this. He'd been with the resort on and off since it was the Belleza Inn back in the 1950s. He'd been good friends with Kim's grandfather Don, and Kim regarded him as part of the family. Even though he could long since have retired, Jonah loved tending bar and listening to folks' stories.

"Jack, I would like to introduce you to Jonah Grady." Kimberly smiled across at her dear family friend, who was dressed in his usual tuxedo shirt with a bow tie and a plaid vest. She'd tried unsuccessfully to get him to dress like the other bartenders but it was a losing battle.

He'd been doing it that way for years and wasn't about to stop now. "He's been a permanent fixture at the Belleza since its inception."

"Nice to meet you." Jack offered Jonah his hand over the small bar and Jonah shook it with aplomb.

"Pleasure to meet you, Mr. Scott."

Jack's brow furrowed. "How do you know my name?"

Kimberly smiled. "Jonah knows everyone's name at the tasting dinner. He makes a point of it every month."

Jonah shrugged. "It's a habit. Makes folks feel at ease."

"It sure does," Jack said. "So what's your best drink, Jonah? I know you have a specialty and I would like one of them."

"Oh, I have something up my sleeve." Jonah reached behind him for a glass. He tossed it in the air and caught it with his other hand. Then he began filling it with ice and then added several liquors and fruit juices. He shook them up in a shaker and then poured his creation into a frosted martini glass and handed it to Jack. "Care to try it?"

"Ladies first." Jack offered Kimberly the glass. At first she seemed hesitant to accept, but she took a sip and then licked her lips.

"Delicious as always, Jonah." She handed the glass back to Jack, who wasted no time taking a sip. When he licked his lips the same as she did, Kimberly felt a tingle deep in her belly.

"I like it. Thank you, sir." He shook Jonah's hand. "You have a gift."

Jonah chuckled. "As do you." He waggled his eyebrows at them. "Y'all have fun tonight."

Jaxon was impressed with the dinner. As each course came out, Gabrielle announced each dish and talked about her inspiration. He couldn't help but notice that they all contained ingredients that were known aphrodisiacs. Was that on purpose? Had Kimberly ensured they had a sexy meal? If so, she needn't have worried because he was damn turned on just sitting next to her. He'd have no problem in that department if that was where the night led.

Even though Kimberly was general manager and should have sat at the head of the table, Robyn had graciously done the honors, leaving Kimberly free to sit next to Jaxon.

Conversation flowed from the senator's current campaign to the movie the A-list actress had just filmed, to gossip about Cole, the R & B singer at the table.

"Did you really date Tea Delgado?" the actress asked him. "It's all over TMZ."

"I don't like to kiss and tell," Cole started to explain, but then he stopped when the waitress came to refill his water glass. "This doesn't have enough ice cubes. I like really *cold* water." He handed her the glass and brushed her off. "Can't people get things right?"

The actress laughed.

Jaxon hated new money. Sometimes the newly wealthy had a tendency to look down on or treat others with no respect. It was the one thing his grandparents had always instilled in him. Money didn't entitle him to be treated better than others.

"Why don't you finish the story?" Jaxon urged. He gave Kimberly a wink because he could see that she, too, had been uncomfortable at the exchange, especially since the young woman was her staff.

Cole went on to regale them with a wild and crazy story of sex and drugs that Jaxon wouldn't believe if he hadn't heard it himself. When Cole's story was over and the dessert course had arrived, Jaxon switched topics. He had a question for the CEO at the table.

"Can you tell us how the IPO is going?" he inquired as he sank his spoon into the creamy mixture.

He'd chosen the lemon-vanilla crème, while Kimberly had opted for the chocolate ganache. "Would you like a taste?"

"I—"

She never finished her sentence because Jaxon slid his spoon into her mouth. She grasped his hand and he gave her a look that made his intentions clear. He wanted her.

She swallowed, but didn't turn away from his gaze until the waitress asked Kimberly if she wanted coffee. "No, thank you."

Jaxon hadn't meant to be so obvious with his desire for her. Perhaps it was the oyster appetizer dish or the pomegranate in the salad or the fig-inspired entrée, but he was very aware of Kimberly. He wanted to spend time alone with her without any interruption.

"That about does it for me," Jaxon said to the senator to his right. "I think I'll go for a stroll on the grounds and walk off this meal."

Kimberly took the cue and rose to address the guests. "It's truly been another great dinner. Let's give one final toast to the executive chef, Gabrielle, before we conclude this month's tasting dinner."

The diners all raised their wineglasses and toasted Gabrielle at the far side of the table. "To the chef."

Jaxon rose from his seat and pulled back Kimberly's.

The buxom blonde he'd seen earlier came barreling through the door. "Kimberly, if I could have a word… There's been an incident."

Gabrielle intervened. "Charlene, why don't you come with me to the kitchen so we can talk?"

He saw Kimberly mouth her thanks to her friend before they said their pleasantries to Robyn and the other guests. Eventually they were finally able to escape the ballroom.

Jaxon opened the door so Kimberly could precede him out of the restaurant, allowing him a great view of her behind in the slinky dress she wore. It was a view he'd never tire of.

Kimberly strolled with Jack through the Plaza's lush surroundings to the main lawn that overlooked a waterfall feature. The lights let off a soft glow and the moonlight set a very romantic scene. *Are we supposed to hold hands?* She planned to keep her hands at her sides, but Jack's large hand reached out and grasped hers. It was a simple gesture, but one that made her uneasy.

Jack made her nervous. He was a risk because he was unlike any of the other men she'd dated. Most of them she'd only *liked*, but Kimberly suspected that Jack would and could make her feel more deeply than that. Right now, he had her feeling hot and lusty. Or was it the humid night air?

"I'm glad we're out of there," he said once they were alone.

"Didn't you enjoy dinner?" Kimberly asked, glancing up at him.

"Very much so," he replied as he looked down at her, "but I would have much preferred dinner alone with you."

Kimberly chose to ignore his comment and make small talk instead. "Then you would have missed out on Gabby's spectacular menu."

"Ah, that brings me to the other interesting part of the evening. Her choice of ingredients."

"I don't understand."

"Oysters, figs, pomegranate, vanilla crème?" He raised a brow. "Those are known aphrodisiacs and heighten the senses. They make you aware of everything and *everyone*."

He stopped walking and turned to her. "And I'm very well aware of you, Kimberly Parker. I've been aware of you and wanting to kiss you for some time now, so I think it's about time I did something about it."

Before Kimberly could protest or deny the very real attraction between them, Jack bent his head and his mouth feasted on hers. The shock of having his lips on hers and feeling his hard, compelling body against her was like a jolt of electricity. She couldn't help but respond by winding her arms around his neck. He took that as an invitation and took more.

His tongue dived inside her mouth and skillfully merged with hers. Stroking her over and over again. His teeth incited wild thrills inside her as he nipped and teased at her mouth. Kimberly responded to his fervent ardor by grasping his head in her hands and allowing him to devour her mouth, because that was the only word she could use to describe the way he ravished her. He took his time drawing out each sensation and she delighted in his warm exploration because it matched her need.

When he finally lifted his head and their lips parted, he said, "That was just as good as I imagined it would be."

How could he talk? Kimberly couldn't speak or put together a coherent thought because she was still trying to catch her breath. Wasn't he just as affected as she was? She turned away and dragged in a deep breath as she touched her swollen lips. She'd felt passion before, but never like this. He must think she was a wanton woman. She spun around on her heel. "If you think you're going to bed with me tonight, then I gave you the wrong impression."

"Did I ask you to bed?"

Kimberly stared back at him in bewilderment. "C'mon, Jack, I know it's what you want."

"You're right," he replied. "I would be lying if I said I didn't want you, Kimberly. I want you in my bed so I can kiss you and touch you all night long. I want to be inside you, make you come and watch you when you do. But I can wait until you're ready for me, until we're both ready to take that next step. Because trust me, after my last relationship didn't end so well, I'm a little gun-shy myself."

Kimberly was at a loss for words. She'd never been spoken to that way before. Jack had just made it very clear how much he wanted her. It was a turn-on, but it also had her running scared.

"You are?" She was surprised by his honesty. Should she be relieved or disappointed that he wasn't about to make a play for her bed?

"Does that surprise you? Not every man is in rush to get a woman into bed. And I certainly wouldn't pressure you."

"That's good to know." Because she certainly wasn't about to jump into bed with a man on the first date.

"But make no mistake about it, it *will* happen." Jack peered down at her. The look in his eyes told her he meant it.

"Why don't I walk you back to your room?" He offered his arm.

"That would be nice."

They walked in a comfortable silence until they made it to her condo. At the door, he pressed her back against the wall and touched his lips to hers again, tasting and deepening the kiss until they were both breathless. His

"Did it really?" Kimberly looked down at her watch in alarm. She hadn't realized she and Jack had been walking that long.

"Yeah, so what took so long?" Gabrielle's eyes were big with excitement.

"Yeah, inquiring minds would like to know," Robyn added.

"We kissed."

"And?" both women simultaneously asked.

"It was the most amazing kiss I've ever had in my life," Kimberly stated unabashedly.

Silent, Gabrielle reached for the ice-cream bucket and took a generous spoonful and put it into her mouth.

It was rare for Gabrielle to be silent, but she hadn't made it a secret that she thought pursuing Jack was a bad idea. And Kimberly understood. Jack had caught her off guard in every way. She hadn't been looking for romance and apparently neither was he, but here they were.

"No one has ever made me feel that way," she said quietly.

"But you let him go to his room alone?" Gabrielle asked.

"Gabby!" Robyn admonished.

"I'm just joking," she responded. "I'm the first one to talk about jumping into bed with someone. I invented the phrase *taking it slow*, but you're entering dangerous territory here, Kimberly."

Robyn nodded. "Gabby's right. Does that mean you're going to put a moratorium on the no-dating-guests policy?"

"No, I think it's a necessary practice," Kimberly said. "But I do feel like a hypocrite when all I want to do is rip his clothes off."

"You're in quite the pickle," Gabrielle said. "What are you going to do?"

Kimberly wished she knew. On the one hand, she knew she should stay away from him and be the example to her staff, but on the other hand, she'd never felt such an instant and strong attraction to a man before. An attraction, she admitted, that she could barely resist.

When Jack had kissed her tonight, if he hadn't pulled away, would she have?

"This is bad," Kimberly said three days later at the staff meeting with all her department heads. The Belleza publicist had just advised her of the fourth bad review of the resort. Over the past two days they'd been posted to major travel sites. It was as though the reviewer purposely went to every travel website to bad-mouth the resort.

"Who do you think could have written them?" Robyn asked.

"I don't know," Kimberly said. "I've gone through all the reservations over the last couple of months and outside of some minor everyday incidents, there have been no complaints of this nature that I wouldn't have been able to address before the guest left the Belleza." She turned to her assistant manager, Antoine. "Can you think of anything?"

Antoine shook his head. "We've had nothing but the highest exit reviews. But the complaints aren't primarily about the hotel." He glanced in Gabrielle's direction.

Gabrielle caught his look and fired back, "You're right, Antoine. They're mainly about The Pearl, or indirectly me. Apparently they're saying that *my* food made them sick."

"Gabrielle, can you think of any incidents over the last couple of months that this could emanate from?"

Kimberly asked. "Any returned plates, food allergies, anything?"

The reviewer had been particularly hard on the food service at the Belleza, claiming the quality of the food was subpar to any other five-star establishments they'd visited. Another review commented that since executive chef Sean Parker's departure a few months ago, the quality of food had gone down.

"No." Gabrielle shook her head. "And I would feel terrible if someone got sick at the hotel from anything that I or my staff may have served."

"Gabrielle, please check with your staff and let's interview all the servers and hostesses. We have to get to the bottom of this before it spirals out of control."

"I'm on it," Gabrielle nodded.

"In the meantime, I've gone onto each of the websites and added a commentary on how we're deeply sorry that we were not able to mitigate the issues during their stay and we'll get to the bottom of the situation, as excellent service is our top priority," Kimberly said.

"What can I do?" Robyn offered.

"Continue on with our next events. And if the bad reviews have leaked through to those clients, reassure them that we will provide the highest quality of service for their event."

"Sure thing."

"We'll circle back at tomorrow's meeting," Kimberly said. "Meeting adjourned." Everyone started to filter out of the room, but as usual Robyn and Gabrielle stayed behind.

Kimberly picked up some of the discarded agendas as she walked around the conference room.

The silence in the room was deafening until Gabrielle asked, "You think this is my fault, don't you?"

Kimberly glanced up. "Of course not. Why would you think that?"

"Because the reviews are primarily aimed at me." Gabrielle pointed to her chest.

"It's probably just a disgruntled employee or something," Robyn offered, patting Gabrielle's back. She could see that this was really bothering her.

"Gabrielle, I know you're a good chef. We all know," Kimberly replied as she continued with her task, "but I have to be impartial and get to the bottom of this."

"What about supporting me?" Gabrielle wailed. "You know I have always followed the proper precautions in my kitchen. I would never harm anyone."

"I know that, Gabby." Kimberly stood up straight. "But I also have an obligation to this hotel to find out the root cause. Please don't take this personally."

"It's pretty hard not to." Gabrielle stalked out of the room in a huff.

"Damn!" Kimberly slammed the papers onto the table. Everything had been going so well over the past six months since she'd taken over running the Belleza and now this. She fell backward into the chair behind her and sighed loudly.

"You were hard on her," Robyn said.

"I had to be!" Kimberly responded. "My family has entrusted this hotel to me, Robyn. The burden is on me if we fail."

"We won't fail, Kim." Robyn came toward her and leaned down until they were eye to eye. "You, we," she said, glancing behind her at the open door Gabrielle had just stormed out of, "have been kicking butt running this place the last six months. Look at all we've done."

"Yes, we have, but we are only as good as our reputa-

'tion and that's the one thing we've always had going for us. Quality and excellent service."

"There will always be naysayers, people ready to bring us down." Robyn reached for Kimberly's hand and gave it a gentle squeeze. "You can't let them get to you. You're stronger than that, Kimberly Parker."

"Thanks, Robyn." She squeezed her hand, grateful for her friend's faith in her. But the niggling doubts continued throughout the day.

Later than night, Kimberly drove over to her parents' house for dinner. She wanted to talk to her parents and get their insight into what could be going on with the bad reviews. She waited until dessert to bring up the topic.

"One or two bad reviews would have been a fluke," she said in conclusion, "but four? That's a record."

"Does sound unusual," her mother, Ilene, replied. "If I had to bet money, I'd put it on your competition."

"The Pinnacle?" Kimberly inquired.

"Logical choice," her mother said. "Wouldn't be the first time a company tried to put another one out of business by bad-mouthing them. My money is on them."

"Sounds pretty sinister, Mama. And not a good way to do business."

Her mother shrugged. "Maybe, maybe not, but you can't have your head in the sand, either. I know you don't have a ruthless bone in your body, baby girl, but there are sharks out there in the water, many of whom would love to take a bite out of an established hotel like the Belleza."

Kimberly thought about it. Her mother could be right and she would certainly look into it, but her father was quiet. "Daddy? What are your thoughts?"

"Oh, I don't think you want to know what I'm thinking," Kurt Parker said.

Kimberly frowned. "Why?" She always trusted his opinion before. What was different now?

"If you have something to say, Kurt, you should just spit it out," her mother said, eyeing him warily. "No need to mince words amongst family."

"All right." Her father sat up straighter in his chair. He clasped his hands together and stared at the two women he loved. "I think it could be Sean."

"What?" Her mother rose from the chair and it crashed to the ground with a resounding thud.

"Daddy!" Kimberly stared back at him in horror, then glanced at her mother.

Ilene Parker was aghast. "Why would you say such a thing, Kurt, let alone think it? That's our son you're talking about."

"Because!" He pounded his fist on the table. "That boy left this house in a huff, furious because *he* didn't get what he felt he deserved, what he thought he was entitled to."

"I know Sean was upset, Daddy," Kimberly responded, "but he would never go this far."

"No?" Her father's voice rose several decibels. "Didn't you say that the reviews are targeting The Pearl? Isn't that where Gabby is executive chef?"

Silence ensued in the room until her father said quietly, "It isn't a stretch to think that the boy would bad-mouth Gabby because she is now executive chef at a restaurant that was once his, that he felt was his birthright."

"I can't hear this." Her mother shook her head. "And I won't. I won't have you accusing my son when he can't defend himself. Sean may not be perfect but he would never hurt the family like this. Never." She stormed out of the room.

Kimberly knew that her mother loved her, but she also

knew that deep down her oldest son, Sean, had always been her mother's favorite. He was a mama's boy, which was why it broke their mother's heart that he was keeping his distance from the family. It probably hurt Sean, too, because he felt as if their mother—the woman who'd always had his back—had betrayed him by backing Kimberly instead of him. Kimberly wished Sean could see how their mother was sticking up for him now.

"I'm with Mama on this, Daddy. There's no way that Sean did this."

Her father shrugged. "If it's not Sean, then it's someone else. Don't be a fool, girl. There's someone out to get you and you'd better have your guard up."

Kimberly drove back to her condo that night, upset not just by the bad reviews but that they had caused a rift between her parents. She hadn't meant to stir the pot by bringing them into this. She'd just wanted some sound advice, but she'd gotten more than she bargained for.

Her father was right about one thing. There was an enemy out to get them. Now she just had to figure out who it was.

Later that night, she knocked on Robyn's condo door. Robyn opened the door with a flourish wearing a lemon-colored silk pajama shorts set.

"Hey, what are you doing here?"

"Can we talk?" Kimberly held up a bottle of Merlot.

"Sure." Robyn motioned her inside. "Come on in."

While Kimberly made herself comfortable on the couch, Robyn went to fetch a wine opener and two goblets. When she returned, she uncorked the wine and poured each of them a glass. "You know this goes against our healthy eating plan." She handed Kimberly a goblet.

"Yeah, but we'll work it off in the gym tomorrow

morning." Kimberly didn't wait for Robyn; she drank liberally.

"Okay, fill me in." Robyn sipped her wine.

"Just left my parents."

"And?"

"We argued."

"Over?"

"Over who could have it out for the Belleza," Kimberly responded, taking another generous sip. "I told them about all the bad reviews. And my father said this has never happened before."

"It's crazy, right?" Robyn tilted her head back for another sip.

"What's crazier is my Dad thinking Sean had anything to do with it!"

"What?" Robyn jumped up off the sofa and began pacing the living room. "How could he think such a thing? Sean would never do something so awful. He may be angry about your father's decision, but he would never bad-mouth the Belleza."

"Whoa!" Kimberly said, holding up her hands in the air in defensive mode. "I never said *I* believed that or that my mom did. We were defending him to my father, but you know how the old man gets when he has his mind made up. And…well, it didn't go well from there. My mother went upstairs in a huff and didn't come down even when I said I was leaving."

Robyn stopped pacing long enough to say, "Of course she's upset. You know Sean is the apple of her eye, just like you're a daddy's girl."

Kimberly smiled. Robyn and Gabrielle knew how close she and her father were. She'd always wanted to be like him. Smart, respected. "Yeah, well, she didn't take too kindly to Daddy thinking ill of her firstborn."

"Speaking of, have you talked to Sean?"

Kimberly shook her head. "He made his choices, plus what would I say?"

Robyn came back and sat on the sofa. "I don't know, but don't you want to heal this rift between the two of you? You guys have always been so close. Don't you miss him? I sure do."

Kimberly glanced at Robyn as fond memories of them hanging together rushed back. She did miss her big brother. He'd always looked after the trio of friends he'd nicknamed "the three amigos." Now there was a void in her life without him. Ryan had always been a loner doing his own thing, but Sean had always been there for her. "I do," she finally answered.

"Then perhaps you should give him a call," Robyn suggested. "You know, make the first move."

"But what if he rejects me?"

"And what if he doesn't? You'll never know if you could make things right between you if you don't try."

Perhaps a call to Sean would heal their relationship and his with the family. Kimberly would give Robyn's advice some serious thought.

Chapter 8

After showering, Jaxon lay back in his bed at his villa. He'd had an intense morning workout and swum several laps in the pool. Yet none of it had been a cure for his Kimberly blues. He hadn't seen her in three days. She hadn't been poolside having breakfast with her friends and when he'd gone to the gym at what he thought was her usual workout time, he'd found it empty. He'd tried calling her office several times but was told she was busy. He'd even left messages, which she hadn't returned.

Was she avoiding him? Had he come on too strong when he'd kissed her the other night after the tasting dinner? He hadn't disguised the fact that he was interested in her—no, make that intensely attracted to her—and wanted her in his bed. But he'd also thought he'd made it clear that he'd wait until the moment was right. Had he misread her signals? Even though she'd been as initially reluctant to pursue their attraction as he'd been, she *had* kissed him back that night. No, she'd more than kissed him. She'd *responded* to him. He remembered feeling her nipples harden against his chest and her arms wind around him.

Was she upset that he hadn't been more aggressive? Kimberly didn't strike him as the dominatrix type, but perhaps he was wrong. Didn't matter anyway. He was out of sorts—all because it had been days since he'd seen a five-foot-seven beauty with legs for miles.

He had to take action. He wouldn't, couldn't let this go. Deep down he knew Kimberly Parker was a special woman and he had to see her again. Resolved, he rose naked from his bed to get dressed and find his woman.

Kimberly was in a foul mood. She hadn't gotten a good night's sleep. Last night she'd tossed and turned in bed. Images of her parents fighting had done little to soothe her spirit, and to top it all off, she'd had a sexy dream about Jack again. It had felt so real that when she'd awoken, she'd been extremely horny and her panties had been damp. Unable to ease her stress, she'd finally taken a shower.

Now it was time for action. All night she'd given thought to Robyn's advice to call her brother Sean. This morning she'd come to the conclusion that she would be the bigger person, that she would reach out to him and try to heal the discord in the family. But when she'd called his cell number, a woman had answered.

Disconcerted to hear a woman on the line, Kimberly had taken several seconds before she spoke. "Umm, may I speak to Sean, please?"

"May I tell him who's calling?"

"It's Kimberly," she replied. "His sister."

She could hear lots of noise in the background. Construction perhaps on his new restaurant? She heard the woman clearly yell to her brother that his sister, Kimberly, was on the phone. Then she'd heard his distinct masculine voice say, "I'm busy. Take a message."

And her heart sank. He'd known it was her and he was refusing to take her call. Darn it! She'd gathered all her willpower to pick up the phone, even when she felt *he* should be the one apologizing to her. She'd tried to be the bigger person by offering an olive branch and he was rejecting her. It was a slap in the face!

She ended the call before the woman could get back on the phone and relay her brother's "get lost" message. He needn't worry. She'd gotten the message loud and clear and she was done being a pushover. If he wanted to behave like a child, then so be it. She was so angry she could spit nails and now she had to deal with the bad reviews.

And that was when she ran into the object of her nightly fantasies as he came strolling toward her in the Plaza.

"Jack!"

"There you are," he said, smiling as his eyes roamed over her. "You've been a hard woman to catch up to these days."

"I'm sorry. I've had a lot of hotel problems to address," she replied smoothly.

"Is everything okay?"

"Yes, why?"

"Well, I've been getting the ice treatment from you and I have no idea why," he responded, "especially after the dinner the other night. I thought we were in a good place."

"Do you think that entitles you to know my innermost thoughts?" she hissed.

Jack held up his hands. "Whoa! Whoa! I don't know where all this hostility is coming from because I certainly don't deserve it. I was actually coming to see if you might want to go off property for the day, but I'll rescind that invitation before it's offered." He turned to walk away, but Kimberly called after him.

"Jack, wait." She rushed toward him in her Prada pumps.

He stopped, but only to say, "If you want another whipping boy, perhaps you should find one of your staff. At least they are paid to take the abuse."

"Touché," Kimberly said. "I'm sorry." She touched his arm. When he glanced down, she quickly removed her hand. "Truly sorry," she added. "I'm having a bad day— hell, a bad few days—and I took it out on you. I'm sorry."

His posture softened and he smiled at her. "All right, that's better. Care to tell me what's going on?"

"I don't know where to begin."

"How about we go to the spa?" he offered. "We could take a refreshing dip in the indoor pool in the solarium and you could unwind a bit."

"During the middle of the day?"

"Why not?"

"Because I'm supposed to be working and—"

He cut her off. "And work will be there when you're done. C'mon." He tugged her arm. "Let's go."

Even though she had work piled high on her desk, Kimberly desperately needed to find an outlet to release some of her stress. Why not play hooky and go off with Jack for a few hours? What could it hurt? When they were done, she could go back and put in a few more hours at her desk.

"Okay, okay," she said, "but I'll have to swing by my condo so I can change clothes. Can I meet you there?"

"See you in twenty."

Jaxon was already in the water in the solarium when Kimberly arrived. Apparently her other guests were enjoying the other amenities as they had the indoor pool and hot tub all to themselves. He was happy he was already in the pool because when she sauntered in wearing a leopard-print bikini, he instantly felt his erection swell in his swim shorts. Luckily the water would keep him cool, or so he hoped.

Kimberly looked like a goddess. The skimpy bathing suit showed him all he'd known was underneath those business suits she wore. He saw full breasts, generous hips and long legs. Even though she'd pulled her hair into a bun, she still looked hot as hell. He couldn't wait to loosen the knot and let her hair fan out around her. He groaned inwardly. He was going to have a hard time keeping his hands off her.

She stepped into the pool. "Ah, this water feels awesome." She threw her head back, allowing the water to wash over her before she popped back up. "This was a great idea and exactly what I needed. Thank you."

"You're welcome," Jaxon said as she swam toward him. "So you wanna tell me what had you so fired up before?"

"Family, work, you, all of the above."

"Me?" He smiled. "Now that's an interesting thought and we'll get back to me in just a moment. Why don't you tell me about your family? What's going on?"

"It's actually work and family entwined together."

"How so?"

"Out of the blue the Belleza recently got some bad reviews within the last few days."

"Has this happened before?"

"Hardly ever," she replied. "We rarely get one bad review online, but four back-to-back? It's unheard of."

"Sounds like sabotage."

"Exactly!" Kim pointed to Jaxon as she trod water. "And that's what I told my parents. But that wasn't what stirred the pot."

"What did?"

"My father accused my brother Sean of posting the bad reviews."

"Your brother who left the resort because you were named general manager?" Jaxon asked.

"You have a good memory."

He hadn't forgotten when she'd confided some of her family troubles to him during their first encounter by the pool. "I do. But why would your father think that?"

Kimberly shrugged. "I don't think my father appreciated having his decision second-guessed and, well, let's just put it this way, he's now in the doghouse by accusing Sean. My mother refuses to speak to him."

"That's her baby boy," Jaxon said. "Mothers get defensive over their cubs."

"To the say the least," Kimberly said. "Anyway, I have to figure out who has it out for the Belleza."

"Let me know if there's anything I can do. I know how hard it can be recovering from a media disaster."

"You do?"

Jaxon nodded. "I've been misrepresented in the media recently and it's caused me some hardship, which is why I'm here at the Belleza lying low." Kimberly stared hard at him and he could see the wheels of her mind turning. "I'm not in any trouble or running from the law. I'm just tired of constantly having to defend myself or being pushed into things I don't want to do. I'm actually a very up-front kind of guy."

At her dubious expression, he said, "Let's get out of this pool. I'd love to chill in the hot tub."

"Oh, okay," she said.

He could see she wanted to know more, ask more questions, and he would comply, but first he wanted Kimberly in a more comfortable setting so he could tell her exactly what was going on with him. She was a trustworthy person and his intuition told him he could tell her his secrets.

She swam over to the steps and Jaxon followed her. He purposely let her go ahead of him so he could check out her butt as she walked up the steps of the pool and sauntered over to the hot tub. He tried to focus and not think about her rear end, but she was wearing the hell out of that leopard-print bikini.

Eventually, they both sank into the swirling bubbles of the hot tub. Jaxon sat on one end and Kimberly sat on the other. He wished she wasn't so far away. Then he could act on the lascivious thoughts he was having about her, like removing that bathing-suit top.

"You realize that's the most you've shared about yourself since we've met," Kimberly said, breaking into his thoughts as she leaned her head back to allow the jets to reach her lower back.

Jaxon blinked. "I—I'm sorry about that," he replied. He knew he'd not been forthcoming with information about himself, but if Kimberly was willing to share her world with him even though she had doubts about getting involved, he at least owed her his story. "That wasn't fair, but I want to be honest now. I want you to know more about me. How about we start with my name." He offered her his hand from across the hot tub. "Jaxon Scott Dunham."

Kimberly's eyes flew open. "What did you just say?"

"You heard right," Jaxon replied. "Jack is short for Jaxon and it's the nickname my family uses."

"The Dunham family," Kimberly added, sitting upright. "Why didn't you say something before now? You let me go on and on about impressing your family."

"I didn't say anything because my family and I are estranged at the moment, much like you and your brothers."

She frowned. "You are? Why?"

"My parents interfered in my life. They tried to force me into a relationship with a longtime family friend who *they* thought was right for me."

"Because she came from the right background?" Kimberly surmised. "Care to tell me about it?"

Jaxon nodded. "I began casually dating Stephanie because it's what my parents wanted. I knew they wanted me to get married but I thought that our dating would appease them for a while. Plus, Stephanie seemed as though she was on board with the arrangement. I was wrong. After a few months of dating, my parents announced to the press that Stephanie and I were getting married."

"Without talking to you?"

"Yep, and when I went to Stephanie to figure out how to get ourselves out of the pickle, I found out she'd been in cahoots with my mother the entire time. I guess she thought she could change my mind and when that didn't work she began sullying my name in the media. Calling me every name you can possibly think of. I didn't lead her on, Kimberly. I swear I made it clear to her from the start that I wasn't interested in marriage."

"That's terrible," she responded. "I can see why you've been staying here for weeks."

"I was so angry with my parents and their role in this entire debacle that I packed my bags and left the family estate in Beverly Hills and came here to the Belleza. I'd heard great things about your hotel. I checked in under an assumed name because I didn't want my family to get wind of where I'm staying. So there, that's the whole sordid mess."

Kimberly smiled. "It's not so sordid, but I'm glad that you finally felt like you could confide in me and, most important, tell me your *real* name."

"You're welcome. I just ask you one favor. My family has no idea where I am and I'd like to keep it that way, if that's all right with you."

"Of course, I would never betray your confidence."

Jaxon suspected she was talking to him as a guest but he hoped she thought of him as more than that. "I know. And I just want you to know that I've been lobbying hard for the Belleza to get the Dunham gala."

"You have? How so?"

"Even though I'm not physically at the board meetings, I dial in remotely and I can express my opinion like any other board member." At her curious expression, he continued, "Each member of my family has a seat on the Dunham Foundation board and a vote. And if I have anything to say about it, you'll get the business."

"Only if you think we're the best," Kimberly replied.

"I know what I like *and* what I want." His gaze dropped from her eyes to her shoulders to her breasts.

"And what's that?"

"I want you," he said unequivocally. He watched her eyes grow large and heavy-lidded. "Matter of fact, I want you right now." He walked over to her and stepped between her open legs.

"Jaxon—" She tried to move, but there was no escape; he had her blocked in.

"I don't know what the future holds, Kimberly. Can't you live in the moment and just *be* with me?"

Kimberly was taken aback by the words coming out of Jaxon's mouth. She knew the risk he'd taken by coming clean with her about who he was, his family and the tabloids who were smearing his name. But they'd just gone from zero to one hundred in the span of five minutes and she needed to slow down the pace before they combusted.

She pushed against the solid expanse of his chiseled chest and asked him one question. "Why did you tell me everything?"

"Because you've opened up to me about your family and I wasn't being equally forthcoming. And quite honestly, this secret life isn't me. I wanted to be real with you, full disclosure, before things went any further between us."

"And what do you see happening between us?"

One of his massive arms reached around her, pulling her to her feet and mere inches from his mouth. "What I see right now is a woman I can talk to, confide in without fear of recrimination, and you can do the same. I see a woman I want to *be* with."

Kimberly was stunned by the smoldering flame she saw in his eyes and the implication sent waves of excitement surging through her. It had been a long time since a man had offered her support of any kind. The ordeal with her brother and the stress of work had taken a toll on her and for the first time in God knew how long she really wanted a man. But if she wanted to get close to Jack—Jaxon—she was going to have to let down her guard. He wasn't offering marriage or commitment, but her intuition told her that Jaxon would never hurt her. And making love with him would be the closest thing to heaven she would ever experience on earth.

"Do you wanna get out of here?" she whispered huskily.

"Hell, yes!"

They quickly climbed out of the hot tub and dried themselves off, and she wrapped her waist in a sarong. While Jaxon grabbed his wallet sitting on one of the lounge chairs. They made it to Kimberly's condo in record time. She didn't even bother to look around her to see if anyone was around. She could think of nothing she wanted more than to be with Jaxon Dunham.

Kimberly fumbled with the key card to her door, unable to insert it into the slot. Jaxon did it for her and opened the door. She walked inside the foyer, but he stayed outside.

"Ask me in."

She did so by wrapping her arms around his neck and pulling him inside. They fell back against the closed door and he swept her up, capturing her mouth with his. He teased at the seams of her lips until she opened willingly to his greedy tongue. She arched against him, pressing her body urgently against his in a whiplash of lust.

"You're so beautiful," he murmured, lifting his head momentarily before covering hers again. His lips were more demanding this time as he explored her mouth. His tongue dived inside, exploring every crook and crevice. It was as if he wanted to devour her whole. As he kissed her, his hands came behind her to untie the halter bikini top she wore and release her breasts from their confines.

His lips left hers to sear a path down her neck and shoulders until he came to one pert brown nipple, anxious for his tongue. Before taking the bud in his mouth, he wet his lips as if he was about to take part in the best meal of his life, and then his mouth closed over her breast.

"Oh!" Kimberly's head fell backward as Jaxon had his way with one breast, then the other. He tasted, teased, licked and fondled her breasts until her knees were weak, but he didn't stop there. He gripped one of her thighs and then slipped his palm underneath her sarong to her bikini bottoms and pushed them aside.

Her breath caught in her throat as Jaxon slid one finger inside her. He moved and swirled it inside her, causing her whole being to flood with desire. With each stroke, she felt passion inching through her veins.

"I want you to come for me here, right now, Kimberly."

"I—" She couldn't think; his fingers were sending pleasure jolts straight through her, but his mouth and tongue hadn't left her breasts. Instead they were sending her on a sensuous path to ecstasy of the most profound kind.

"Tell me you want me," he said as a second finger surged inside her. His voice was throaty and breathless with passion.

Kimberly couldn't speak because Jaxon was ravishing her right there in the hallway of her condo. They hadn't even made it to the bed yet. His two fingers slid in and out of her womanly center, making her horny as hell. Who was he that he could make her feel this way? Make her behave so shamelessly?

"Tell me you want this," he urged.

"I want this… I want you, Jaxon." She arched her body toward him, eager for more of his fingers, of his mouth, of Jaxon.

His fingers became more insistent and Kimberly could feel him tipping her over the edge fast. His mouth moved from her breasts back to her mouth. His tongue mimicked the motion of his fingers deep inside her, causing Kimberly to fragment into a million pieces.

"Jaxon!" She clutched his shoulders, clinging to him for support.

When the eruptions began to subside, he swept her up in his arms and began walking toward the back of her condo.

"Where's your bedroom?" he grumbled.

"Next door." She could barely manage the words as Jaxon kicked the door open and walked over to her large king-size platform bed and placed her half-naked body on the comforter.

"I'll be right back."

Kimberly had no idea where he was going. She didn't have to wait long because he returned with two large candles from her living room and lit each one. Then he closed the drapes, blocking the sunlight so they had only the flicker of the candlelight to illuminate the room.

She soon smelled the sweet scent of lavender and honey wafting through the air, but nothing was more fragrant than the manly scent of Jaxon as he approached the bed. He looked at her and she could see the desire in his eyes. She recognized it because it mirrored her own. She rose on her haunches and moved like a panther toward him until she met him at the foot of the bed.

He closed the gap between them and they reached for each other simultaneously. She melted when he kissed her. It was an impossibly tender kiss, drawing her in. Then his kiss grew urgent and insistent and her arms twined like a rope around his neck, pulling him forward until they fell back onto the bed, a mass of legs and arms. Kissing, touching, tasting each other.

"I want to make you feel good. May I?" he asked.

"Yes, yes, make me feel good," she whispered. Kimberly couldn't remember if ever a man had made her feel so alive, so wanted, so desired. She wanted Jaxon badly.

He trailed a blaze of hot kisses along the base of her neck, jawline and cheek before slowly moving back to her mouth and taking it with an intensity that took her breath away. He thrust his tongue deep inside her mouth. He rubbed his palms over her nipples. His hands weren't rough, but rugged like a man's hands should be, and she welcomed his possessive caress. Her nipples perked at his touch.

His mouth left hers and moved to her neck. When he found her sensitive spot, he stayed there sucking her and

Kimberly just knew she would have a love mark tomorrow to prove it, but she didn't care. She wanted more of his tongue. "Yes, oh…yes," she moaned, urging him on.

Jaxon returned to his earlier ministrations and took the turgid buds of her breasts in his mouth. He alternated between sucking and teasing them with quick flicks of his tongue, but she didn't complain; she was loving every minute of it. Jaxon was the first man in years to make her feel like a woman. When she felt his tongue move lower from her breasts to her stomach, she jumped slightly. He was at her belly button, teasing it ever so subtly, and Kimberly felt like a giddy schoolgirl being touched for the first time. But she wasn't. She was a grown woman in need of his touch, so she didn't shy away when she felt his breath at the junction between her thighs.

He quickly removed the bottom half of her bathing suit as he'd done with her top earlier. He kissed her inner thighs before reaching her moist folds. Kimberly held her breath waiting for what she knew was to come. He hovered over her, heightening her awareness of what he was about to do her, and when he finally dived his tongue inside her wet heat, she rose high off the bed. Jaxon was masterful with his tongue, lapping at the folds of her wet center.

Kimberly grasped hold of his head, holding him in place as she relished every wicked thing he was doing to her. But he didn't use just his mouth; his fingers soon joined his agile tongue and slipped inside her. She could feel both his tongue and finger simultaneously inside her and she knew she wouldn't be able to hang on much longer.

Jaxon didn't want Kimberly to hold back with him. He'd sensed her nerves when they'd made it back to her condo. She was skilled at hiding them, but he could see through it.

He wanted her to break for him, to cry out his name, and she had. He'd already made her orgasm once and he was looking forward to making her come a lot more before the day was over. He was greedy, needy and anxious to have her open for him. He couldn't wait for her to wind those sexy legs of hers around him so he could do with her as he liked and in any way he wanted. Kimberly was a woman used to being in control, but right here, right now, he was in control.

He thrust his tongue deeper inside her and heard her moan in delight. "Yes, babe," he urged. He wanted to hear that she was enjoying what he was doing to her. And she was, because she moaned softly.

Again, he thrust deep, in and out, until he began to feel her muscles contract. He grasped both of her hands that had once held his head in place and put them to her sides while he took full advantage of her and brought her to climax.

Kimberly cried out his name as her thighs quivered around his face. "Jaxon!"

Her head fell backward against the comforter and Jaxon slid upward until he could brush his lips across her. He could still taste her on his lips and she tasted so good that he couldn't wait for another go-round, but first he needed to be inside her.

Before she could recover from her second orgasm, he pulled down his swim shorts and tossed them onto the floor, but not before removing a condom from his wallet, which also held his hotel key card. Intuitively, he'd known that they were headed for this moment and had come prepared. He sheathed himself, protecting them, and then moved over her.

He brushed her hair aside and grasped both sides of her face. "Look at me."

She blinked her eyes, bringing him into focus.

"Do you know how beautiful you are? How much I want you?"

"As much as I want you," she whispered, staring into his eyes. It was exactly what he wanted to hear.

"Good!" Jaxon took her mouth just as the lower half of his body spread her legs wide. He settled himself between her thighs and surged forward toward the soft curls of her feminine entrance.

He watched her pupils dilate as her body began to accommodate him. She was wet, but tight. He was surprised just how tight she was, but it felt good. He thrust his hips and sank deeper inside her. She felt so good around him! He eased in and out of her with a slow and steady pace as she lay pinned beneath him. He lifted her off the bed and he squeezed her tight butt, bringing her into closer contact with his bulging erection.

"Jaxon…" She wrapped her legs around his hips, drawing him deeper inside her body.

"Yes, love?"

"Harder," she said, looking at him as he thrust inside her. "Faster…please."

He answered her request by increasing the tempo, giving her exactly what they both wanted. She moaned aloud each time he drove into her.

Had Kimberly put some spell on him? He was lost in the sensation of being inside her as he rode them into oblivion. He knew today was just a promise of what was to come and an animal growl of pleasure escaped his lips. He was swamped in a need to devour her whole. He pumped faster, wilder, and then withdrew before filling her again. A guttural groan escaped his lips when her climax made her inner muscles clench around him, triggering his own release.

He collapsed on top of her and felt their sweat mingled together, but Kimberly didn't seem to mind. Quickly he rolled to his side, pulling her next to him. He didn't want to lose the connection they'd just shared. Before he fell asleep in her arms, he had one last thought. How was it that no other woman had ever made him feel this way?

Chapter 9

Kimberly awoke with a start, but not before she felt a hairy leg covering her thigh. She glanced to her side and saw Jaxon's sleeping face on her pillow. Remembrance came flooding back to her of her wanton behavior that afternoon. She'd never been into casual hookups, let alone with a guest of the hotel. She'd broken every one of her cardinal rules by sleeping with Jaxon, especially when he'd made it pretty clear that he wasn't interested in commitment, but she'd been unable to resist his charms. He was all broad shoulders and breathtaking beauty. His muscles even gleamed in the sunlight streaming through the drapes of her condo.

This afternoon when she'd run into Jaxon, she'd been in a bad temper, but talking to him had allayed some of her fears. Jaxon seemed to understand her like no one else did, not even Robyn or Gabrielle and certainly not Ben Lawson. Jaxon must have felt the same way because he'd finally opened up to her and shared some of himself with her.

And making love with Jaxon—well, that had just rocked her world. She hadn't been prepared for the intensity of her attraction to him or how he would make her respond. She was surprised no one had heard them, given that he'd made her scream out his name as she came.

He was just so darn sexy, it was hard not to give in to every carnal desire that had lived in her fantasies. Something told her that Jaxon wouldn't mind fulfilling every single one of them.

Jaxon rolled over and caught Kimberly staring at him. Her usually sleek black hair was tousled, her lips were plump and swollen from his demanding kisses, and if he wasn't mistaken he could see a love mark forming on her neck. She'd tasted so good, he hadn't been able to control himself. He'd wanted to taste every inch of her body and he had. They'd just had the most mind-blowing sex he'd ever had. After he'd been thinking and dreaming about her for days, she had lived up to his expectations, so much so that he'd promptly fallen asleep after their lovemaking.

"Hey," he said, reaching out to stroke her hair.

"Hi yourself."

"That was, uh…" He struggled for the words.

"Amazing?"

"Mmm…"

"Incredible?"

He nodded his agreement.

"Exciting? Thrilling?"

"Oh, yes…"

"Ready for another round?" she asked, pushing him onto his back and swinging her leg over his waist so she could straddle him.

"What do you think?" He lifted his upper body and kissed her mouth, her face and her throat. He loved the sensation of having her breasts against his naked chest. He wanted more and Kimberly gave it to him.

Instead of taking him inside her as he'd anticipated, she slid down on the bed. Then she reached for his throbbing manhood and wrapped her fingers around him and slowly began sliding her hands up and down his engorged flesh. Jaxon could barely withstand the slow, steady motion as she explored every inch of him from his blossoming shaft to the tip of his penis. He couldn't wait for her mouth to be on him.

"You don't play fair," he groaned when she began to quicken her pace with rapid strokes.

"Fair's no fun," she murmured, glancing up at him before taking his penis fully inside her mouth.

Jaxon leaned back against the bed and let Kimberly stroke, tease and lick him with her tongue until he began to groan. He didn't want to come, not until he was inside her, but Kimberly was tempting him to climax.

"Baby," he moaned.

"Yes?"

"Baby, stop, I want to be inside you. I need to be."

She looked up at him, a wicked grin lighting her face that told him the pleasure was only getting started.

Kimberly loved the feel of Jaxon as she'd manually and orally stimulated him. He'd felt hot and throbbing and she'd looked forward to giving him as much pleasure as he'd given her. And now she was about to get some of her own. She reached for the packet of condoms lying near the edge of the bed and slid one onto Jaxon. Then, before he had time to think or move, she sat atop him and took him deep inside her.

A burst of pleasure surged through her at having him fill her so completely. Jaxon pulled her head down so he could deepen their kiss as they moved together, kissing, stroking, touching each other as one unit. He held her gaze as she undulated against him, moving faster and faster against him. He held her hips as her pelvis slammed against him and she rode him like a horse.

Kimberly could feel herself being swept away, could feel her orgasm coming on, but she didn't want this moment to end. Her need for him consumed her. Having Jaxon inside her felt so good, so right. But the pressure inside her was building and she could no longer stave off the eruption. She exploded with a cry and he bucked underneath her as he groaned aloud.

Spent, she collapsed against him and her hair fanned out over his chest. Had his world fragmented as hers had?

Eventually, after making love one more time, they made it out of bed. Kimberly wrapped her silk robe around her and went into the kitchen in search of sustenance. Jaxon, however, sauntered in buck naked without a care in the world. Kimberly glanced at the clock on the stove and was horrified when she realized it was nearly dinnertime.

Where had the time gone? She'd been so wrapped up in Jaxon that she hadn't made it back to the office. She felt guilty considering all the resort had going on right now. She should be looking into the bad reviews instead of making love with Jaxon all afternoon, but it had felt so good to be bad.

She glanced in her refrigerator. There wasn't much in the way of edible contents except some 2 percent milk, a four-pack of yogurt, a platter of cheese and fruit from an event earlier that week, and several bottles of water. She was turning around when she slammed right into Jaxon's naked, solid body. He began nuzzling her neck, which almost made her forget her reason for coming into the kitchen.

"I'm sorry there isn't much food." She pulled out the platter and slid out of his grasp to place it on the counter.

If she didn't, he'd be backing her against the counter and taking her right there in the kitchen. *That isn't a bad idea*, her inner voice said. But she was also rather hungry.

She pulled the plastic wrap off the platter, grabbed a couple of grapes and threw them into her mouth.

Jaxon joined her and ate several cubes of the Monterey Jack cheese. "What do you say we order some real food? We can eat in."

"You mean to tell me you don't like my selection?" Kimberly asked with a smile.

"Babe, I need real food that sticks to your bones. I don't think we'll survive the night on this." He eyed the sparse platter.

"The night?" Kimberly raised an eyebrow. "Who said you could stay the night?"

Jaxon stopped his nibbling and headed straight toward her. He drew her to him until her breasts were flattened against his chest and then he backed her up against the sink. She could feel his manhood pressing against her thighs because her Victoria's Secret robe reached only her midthigh.

Without a word, he pulled at the tie on her robe until it fell open, leaving her naked to his admiring gaze. He reached behind her, grasped her behind and pulled her to his throbbing erection. Warmth began to spread to her thighs and he hadn't even entered her.

"You want me to leave?" he asked, pressing into her. She could feel the tip of his manhood hovering at her opening and she was becoming wet. How was it possible after they'd already made love too many times to count this afternoon?

She shook her head, unable to speak. She couldn't think when he was standing this close to her. All she could think of was having him inside her. She needed him inside her.

"Then ask me to stay," he ordered as he lifted her off her feet.

She had no choice but to wrap her legs around him and answer, "Jaxon, please stay. I want you to stay."

A triumphant smile spread across his full lips. She knew he wanted to take her right then and there, but they needed protection. "Condom?" she asked.

"I'll be right back." He lowered her to her feet and headed in the direction of her bedroom.

She would have thought he would have carried her back to their afternoon love nest, but instead he returned a few moments later with a condom already on. There was a hungry look in his gaze as he rushed for her, picking up where they'd left off.

"I'm going to take you right here and make you come until I'm done with you." He lifted her off her feet again and she complied by wrapping her legs around him seconds before his hard arousal thrust inside her. He sat her on the counter and began hammering into her.

"Oh, my!" Kimberly let out a loud sigh as Jaxon pumped inside her with delicious strokes. In and out and in and out again.

Jaxon was crazy with lust for Kimberly and he smothered her mouth with a ravenous kiss. He suckled on her bottom lip until she opened her mouth for him. He dived inside and tasted her fully. He hadn't intended on making love to her on the kitchen counter. But when she'd jokingly said he might not be welcome for the night, he'd wanted to show her the intensity of their attraction for each other. There was no way he was leaving. He didn't know what it would take before he was sated, but Kimberly was like a drug and he couldn't get enough.

Her inner muscles clenched around him, tightening around his erection, milking him. He wasn't going to last. When he felt her begin to tremble, he came undone. He climaxed inside her, crashing into her with an explosion of pure unadulterated pleasure.

"Kimberly!" He groaned as he slammed into her one final time. He clutched her to him, sucking on one of her breasts as he did.

When the quaking in their bodies began to subside, he lowered her back to the floor.

She glanced up at him with glazed eyes. She had to feel as he did that the passion between them was off the charts.

"Are you okay?" He brushed aside the damp hair that had fallen in her face. "I'm sorry if I was rough with you."

"You weren't," she said, tucking it behind her ear. "A bit unexpected, but not rough."

A light sheen of sweat glistened on her breasts and he reached over to pinch one of her nipples. "Now I'm really starved."

"You and me both. Let's order." She closed her robe as she walked over to a drawer by the stove and pulled out the Belleza menu. "What are you in the mood for?" she asked, glancing in his direction.

"Food and you. In that order."

"Has anyone ever told you you're insatiable?"

"A time or two."

She rattled off several selections and after they'd placed their order, they returned to nibbling on the fruit-and-cheese platter until the food arrived.

"I'm curious," Kimberly said, leaning against the counter. "Where does your family think you are?"

Talking about his family was like a splash of cold water on his arousal. "I don't know. Maybe in the Caribbean somewhere. They know I like the islands. Why do you ask?"

Kimberly shrugged as she reached for a sliced apple and popped it into her mouth. "It's just that you're right under their noses, barely a two-hour drive, and they have no idea."

"And that's the way I'd like to keep it."

She must have recognized his serious tone because she quickly responded, "Of course. I would never betray my guests' privacy."

"After today, am I still just a guest?" Jaxon asked, staring at her.

"Of—of course not," she stammered. "That came out wrong. I would never betray *your* confidence. It means a lot that you shared your story with me."

Relieved, he let out a breath, not just because she'd agreed to keep his secret, but because to him, she was more than just the manager of the hotel he was staying at. She was his lover. "That's because I don't have to pretend to be someone I'm not. I can just be real with you, Kimberly. You don't judge me or have expectations like my family. You like me just as I am."

She grinned up at him and he noticed that she had a small dimple in her right cheek. "I don't just like you, I think you're wonderful," she said.

Her honesty was refreshing and Jaxon knew that he would be staying at the Belleza a lot longer than he'd anticipated. Not only was Kimberly Parker a breath of fresh air, but he hadn't responded in bed to a woman the way he had with her in…well, never. Until he could get her out of his system, he wasn't going anywhere.

Chapter 10

Kimberly skipped her normal workout as Jaxon had helped her burn off more than enough calories during their marathon lovemaking session, which had gone well into the morning. Kimberly had gotten only a few hours of sleep before she'd finally gotten up and showered to prepare for the day. Jaxon was still in bed and she'd told him to stay. He was on vacation, but she was not. After playing hooky yesterday, she needed to be the first one in.

When she'd checked her phone this morning, there had been several texts from the office, Robyn and her parents, but none from Gabby. She knew Gabrielle felt as though she was the scapegoat, but that was far from the case. Yes, Gabrielle was one of her oldest, dearest friends, but Kimberly had to be impartial when they were at the office. And when the evidence pointed to the restaurant, as general manager, Kimberly had to look into it. She just hoped Gabrielle would understand the position she was in. She had to be fair to everyone and not appear as if she was playing favorites, though she knew some of her staff thought that way.

She was able to get through her nearly one hundred email messages, her voice mails and complete a property walk-through before she received a call from Jaxon. "Hey, beautiful."

"Hey, handsome." Hearing his voice made her heart beat wildly.

"How's your day going?"

"Better," Kimberly said and she meant it. She hadn't solved their sabotage problem nor had she forgotten her brother's lack of interest in repairing their relationship, but hearing Jaxon's voice did wonders for her disposition.

"Good. How about dinner tonight?" he asked. "I know a great spot."

"I would love to." She could use a night off property and away from curious eyes. She hadn't told the girls about her night with Jaxon or his true identity. She felt guilty about not being forthright with her friends. They usually shared their sexy stories over their morning work-out and breakfast, but today Kimberly had wanted to keep it to herself for a little while longer. Besides, how could she share her feelings when she didn't understand them herself? Jaxon was making her feel things she'd never felt for another man. He was awakening a side to her that she fully wanted to explore without questioning eyes.

"I'll be at your condo at seven."

Promptly at 3:00 p.m., the department heads began filing into the conference room. Kimberly smiled at Robyn when she entered wearing a fuchsia silk blouse and black pencil skirt and low-heeled sandals. It was just like her to wear bold, bright colors. Gabrielle, however, did not look in Kimberly's direction nor did she look like herself. Her wild carefree curls were in a simple fishtail updo and she was formal in her chef's coat rather than her usual ensemble of jeans and a T-shirt. Kimberly would have to talk to her later and clear the air. She didn't like this hostility between them.

During the meeting, she caught up on the usual items

before turning her focus to Gabrielle. "Any information on your investigation of complaints at The Pearl?"

Gabrielle shook her head. "No." She pulled out several comment cards. "In fact, we've had quite a few positive comment cards placed at the front desk lately when guests have departed saying how much they enjoyed The Pearl. I really have no idea where this stems from."

"I see." Kimberly rubbed her chin. "That's unfortunate. That means that someone is out to sabotage the resort. We're all going to have to be extra diligent in our services here at the resort. I'll take the next steps to look into this matter. Any other new business?"

After the usual updates on reservations, food/beverage and special events, the meeting concluded. Gabrielle rose, but Kimberly beat her to door. "A word?" Kimberly asked.

"I really have to get back," Gabrielle replied, glancing at her watch. "I'm baking fresh baguettes."

"This won't take long and I'm sure your staff can cover for you."

Gabrielle rolled her eyes, but stayed rooted to the spot.

Once everyone had gone and it was just them and Robyn, Kimberly began, "Gabby, listen—"

"Don't Gabby me, Kim." She folded her arms across her chef's coat. "You pulled rank on me yesterday. You don't have to remind me, or Robyn," she huffed and pointed to their friend, who was standing quietly behind her, "that your family owns this establishment. What you do need to do is respect the contribution that we both make."

"You know I do, but—"

"I would never knowingly put your family's business in danger or cover it up, for that matter," Gabrielle responded. "It sickens me to think that my food could have harmed anyone. And I will do my best to ensure it doesn't happen again. You can count on that."

"I know that, Gabby," Kimberly said quietly as she walked toward her. "And I'm truly sorry if I made you feel like I wasn't in your corner. I am and I always will be. But these reviews are serious and could threaten the Belleza and all of our livelihoods. It may seem like I'm harsh at times, but I want—no, I need us to be a success."

"Is this still about proving to your family that they made the right choice?" Robyn jumped into the conversation.

"Robyn..." Kimberly gave her a look. She didn't want her private fears aired.

"What? You don't want to go there?" Robyn asked, folding her arms across her bosom. "Why not? It's what we're all thinking. Heck, your parents think Sean is behind these reviews."

"Sean?" Gabrielle looked confused and glanced back and forth between the two of them. "What does he have to do with any of this?"

Kimberly sighed. "My father accused him of being the culprit behind these bad reviews."

"As much as Sean might be angry with Mr. Parker, he would never sabotage my reputation as executive chef at The Pearl," Gabrielle defended her mentor. He'd taken her under his wing when she'd returned to the States, Kimberly knew. And she was a better chef because of him.

"I know that!" Kimberly snapped. "I don't believe it any more than you do."

"So why are we fighting?" Robyn asked. "Can't we just put this behind us and move on? Kim, you say you're sorry. And Gabby, you stop wearing your heart on your sleeve."

"Well, all right!" Gabrielle sniffed at her reality check.

"I'm sorry if I hurt your feelings," Kimberly offered.

She wanted to put this behind them and move on. She hated being at odds with her friends.

Gabrielle turned her head and was silent for several seconds before turning back around to face her. "And I'm sorry if I took it a little too personally, but it's an affront when my food is criticized."

"Understood." Kimberly offered a half smile. "But I don't think this is about your food. Someone has it out for the Belleza and we need to find out who."

"But how?" Robyn asked.

"You'll see."

After Robyn left, Kimberly set about making some discreet inquiries for a private investigator. She needed to find out the source of these reviews and squelch them once and for all.

The afternoon dragged out for Jaxon. He couldn't get his mind off Kimberly and the night they'd spent together. When he'd awoken later that morning in her bed and reached for her, she'd been gone and his erection had been less than pleased. The woman had woken up the sleeping tiger and he'd been hungry for her ever since. He'd hardly let Kimberly sleep before he'd felt himself getting hard and had to make love to her again earlier that morning. They'd used the entire two packs of condoms he'd brought.

He'd finally showered and dragged himself back to his room to check in at Dunham Investments. After dealing with a few emails and contacting several clients, he called his parents. He needed to keep them under the assumption that he was still out of the country without rousing their suspicions, but when he called the estate, his sister answered.

"Jaxon!" Hayley was nearly out of breath when she picked up the phone.

"Hey, Hales, how are you?"

"I'm fine. And you? Are you enjoying your time away?" she asked. *"Abroad?"*

"Yes, I am. Why?" She sounded suspicious of his whereabouts.

"I was just wondering when you planned on coming home. Without you here Mama has to have someone to fret over and I'm her new whipping boy, or girl."

"Sorry, kid, but I'm not coming home just yet."

"Having too much fun?"

Jaxon laughed and his mind went to that moment yesterday when he'd backed Kimberly up against the counter and had his way with her in the kitchen. It had been incredibly hot and sexy. Just thinking of it now caused his member to swell. "Uh, yeah, something like that."

"I bet." Hayley laughed.

"You sound like you know something."

"Who, me?" Hayley asked. "I keep my head out of other's people's business."

"Perhaps you can remind our parents to do the same."

"You can tell them yourself." A second of silence ensued, followed by her saying, "Mama, Jaxon's on the phone."

Jaxon took a deep breath and girded his loins for the Spanish Inquisition.

"Jaxon, is that you?" Claire Dunham asked on the other end of the line.

"Yes, Mother."

"When are you coming home?"

"Soon?"

"That's not an acceptable answer," his father, Charles,

said, joining the call. "Dunham Investments needs you here."

"I would beg to disagree with you on that," Jaxon replied. "I've spoken with my clients and they are very happy with my services even though I'm not local. I'm meeting my obligations."

"What about your obligation to this family? Your obligation to providing a Dunham heir?"

Jaxon scoffed. It was funny that his father would bring up *his* obligation considering his parents were the ones who'd run him off in the first place. He ignored his father's questions. "I'm calling to check in and let you know I'm fine so you don't worry, but if that's not good enough—"

His father interrupted, "Jaxon, this really has gotten out of hand. I know you were unhappy with how we handled your engagement to Stephanie, but don't you think you've punished us enough? Punished your mother enough?"

Of course he would try to make Jaxon feel guilty, as if he'd done something wrong. "You mean my *arranged* engagement by Mom and Stephanie? Well, I'm not interested and if you persist down this road, I'll make my stay indefinite."

"Are you threatening me, young man?"

"Charles, please," his mother jumped in. "We just want you back home, Jaxon, where you belong. I promise not to interfere in your life again."

Jaxon wished he could believe that, but right now his mother was just telling him what she thought he needed to hear until she got her way. Then she'd be right back to meddling in his affairs. "I'll be home soon. You take care and I'll be on the next Foundation call next week." Seconds later, he ended the call. He refused to get into another debate with his parents on his obligations to the Dunham family.

What he wanted to do was focus on his dinner date with Kimberly and what was to come afterward when he would have his way with her.

Chapter 11

Kimberly debated what to wear for her dinner with Jaxon until it was nearly time for him to arrive. She finally settled on a bronze V-neck peplum top, skinny jeans, chandelier earrings, her favorite stilettos and a clutch. She wanted to wear something sexy rather than the stuffy suits and dresses that Jaxon saw her in most days. She wanted him to see that she was capable of letting her hair down and being carefree.

Though she supposed he may have caught that from the abandoned way she'd behaved in bed the day before. He probably thought her some sex-crazed nympho given that she'd been more than happy to stay in bed with him all day with a break only to eat room service.

She added a gold necklace, since the deep plunge of the top would show off her cleavage. She surveyed herself in her pedestal mirror. She sure hoped Jaxon liked what he saw when she opened the door. She had just sprayed perfume to her wrists, earlobes and cleavage when the bell rang. Her stomach vibrated as if a swarm of bees had gathered there. How could she still be nervous at seeing him considering how intimate they'd been? In actuality, this was their first real date. Most of their encounters centered around the Belleza, but now they were charting new territory.

She opened the door and Jaxon spun around to face her. His dark smoldering gaze sent a shiver up her spine as it surveyed every inch of her. In jeans that hugged his thighs and a purple button-down shirt open at the throat, he looked fine himself.

"You look good enough to eat," Jaxon said as he brushed his soft lips across hers.

"Thank you."

"You ready to go?"

She nodded and grabbed her clutch from the side table. "Yes, I can't wait." She closed the door behind her and locked it. "So where are we going?"

"You'll see." He grasped her hand and together they walked down the stairs to the car he'd rented.

Jaxon had good taste. The silver Jaguar was sleek and sophisticated with a supple leather interior and all the latest technology. He helped her into the passenger seat before going around to the driver's side. But before he turned over the engine, he leaned over to give her another kiss, except this one was longer, deeper and stirring. Kimberly could feel her toes curling in her stilettos. He eventually kicked the engine into gear and they set off. She didn't know where they were going; she just knew she would enjoy whatever it was because she was with Jaxon.

"How was your day today? Any more bad reviews?" he inquired.

"No, thank God," Kimberly replied, "but I still suspect someone is trying to sabotage the resort so I'm hiring a private investigator."

"You think it's that serious?" He hazarded a glance in her direction.

"Could be. I just can't take any chances that this might spiral out of control. I'm trying to cover all my bases."

"I think that's wise, but what about your family?"

"Now that's another story," she responded. "I haven't spoken with my parents since dinner the other night." She turned to Jaxon. "I guess I'm kind of afraid to."

"Are you hoping it's all going to go away? If you're not putting your head in the sand on the Belleza, why are you doing it in this situation?"

"It's different," Kimberly said. "It's personal."

Jaxon nodded. "I hear you."

"I didn't tell you the other reason I was upset yesterday. You see, I tried to reach out to my older brother, Sean."

"And? What happened?"

"He wouldn't even come to the phone. Can you believe that?"

"I'm sorry to hear that, Kim. I know this tension between you two has been weighing heavily on your heart."

"Yeah, but what can I do if he won't even meet me halfway?"

He put a comforting hand on her thigh. "I understand. A reconciliation takes two."

"What about you and your family? Will you ever speak to them again?"

"That's the difference, Kimberly. I have spoken with them. I called them just today, but my parents don't want to take responsibility for their role in the rift that's between us."

Kimberly chuckled bitterly. "We've got problems, don't we?"

Jaxon smiled in her direction. "Nothing that a bottle of good Merlot can't solve, at least for tonight. Why don't we agree to put our problems on the shelf tonight and just enjoy each other's company?"

"Deal."

Kimberly was impressed when Jaxon stopped the Jaguar in front of the valet stand at a Colombian restaurant she'd been hearing great things about for some time, but had never had the time to visit.

The hostess seated them almost immediately in the center of the tropically decorated restaurant with palm trees and Colombian decor lining the walls. A small wooden stage was in front of them.

"What's the stage for?" Kimberly asked as Jaxon pulled out the chair for her to sit down.

"We have flamenco dancers," the hostess answered instead. "The next show is in about thirty minutes."

"Sounds great," Kimberly replied. "Have you been here before?" she asked Jaxon when the hostess departed.

"No, but it was recommended by the Belleza concierge."

Kimberly smiled; her staff was making her proud.

"Wine, sangria or a mojito?" Jaxon asked.

"Mmm…all of those sound wonderful. Since we're in a Colombian restaurant, let's get sangrias."

They perused the menus, talking over options, and while doing, so Kimberly learned that Jaxon spent a summer abroad in Spain, where he gained a love of Spanish cuisine.

When the waiter came over to take their order, bringing with him a basket of Cuban bread, she wasn't surprised when Jaxon spoke fluent Spanish when placing their sangria, tapas and entrée order.

"Were you there as a foreign exchange student or just bumming around Europe?"

Jaxon laughed heartily at her question. "My parents would never have allowed me to just bum around Europe. Wouldn't have gone with the Dunham image. No, I was a student and stayed with this wonderful family who treated me like their own son. I helped teach their three young children English while exploring all that the country had to offer."

"Sounds amazing. I wish I had traveled more when I was young." She tore off a piece of the crusty bread before slathering it with a generous amount of the sweet cream butter.

"What were your summers like?"

"They were spent at the Belleza," Kimberly said, munching the bread. "Learning the business from the ground up."

"Do you regret it?" he asked just as the waiter returned with their sangria. He poured them each a glass of the rich-bodied red wine and citrus juice mixture.

"To us." Jaxon lifted his glass.

"To us." Kimberly clicked his glass with hers and took a sip. "This is delicious."

"Good choice."

"To answer to your earlier question," Kimberly replied, "I don't regret it. It was a great experience learning at my father's feet. I think it's why he chose me to run the resort when he retired. But at times, I do wish I'd been able to be more of a teenager."

"So you've always been this focused, this determined?"

"Yes, and don't get me wrong, it served me well, but while my brother Ryan was able to screw up and make mistakes, my father expected more from me."

She suspected Jaxon understood what it was like to live up to his family's expectations. Wasn't that why he'd left town? "So tell me. What was it like growing up as a Dunham?"

Jaxon joined her and ate some of the Cuban bread as he filled her in on happier moments from his childhood. Like when he and Hayley went skiing for the first time or when they attempted a family camping trip. He didn't want to spend their evening talking about what they wished they had done or on regrets. He wanted it to be fun, so he told her about sneaking out of the house with some friends to go to a bar and getting caught drinking. "I was grounded for a month for underage drinking."

"Sounds like you were quite a handful," Kimberly replied.

"Yeah, I think I drove my mother crazy trying to buck family tradition." Jaxon laughed. "But she couldn't discipline me. She left that to my father."

The waiter brought their entrées of seafood paella and chicken Manchego.

"Your chicken looks delicious," Kimberly said, eyeing the breaded chicken cutlet with Manchego cheese, sun dried tomatoes and basil with yellow rice.

Immediately he cut her a piece and then leaned to place it in her open mouth. Their eyes connected across the table and as Kimberly chewed she could feel the sexual tension stirring between them.

"You like?" Jaxon's dark eyes never left hers.

She paused before eventually saying, "Yes, it's delicious."

Just then, the flamenco dancers took to the stage. One man, dressed in all black, danced with three women all wearing red dresses with flounced skirts and flaming-red flamenco shoes.

They began stomping and kicking their heels as the women used the castanets. It was all very charming and when they asked for volunteers, Jaxon stood up and began pointing to Kimberly.

The dancers came down the stage and headed straight for her. "No, no." Kimberly shook her head, but they wouldn't take no for an answer. They led her to the stage and one of the females began to show her the steps. Kimberly looked down at Jaxon and he was smiling up at her and giving her an encouraging thumbs-up.

Kimberly tried to do the steps and hoped she didn't show off two left feet. After a few minutes, they mercifully walked her back to her table. Everyone in the restaurant gave her resounding applause.

"You were great," Jaxon told her. But Kimberly couldn't speak because standing behind him with a woman was her brother Sean.

Seeing the stunned look on Kimberly's face, Jaxon swiftly turned around to see who or what had caused her such alarm.

"Kimmy, you always did have two left feet," Sean said.

Kimberly stared at her older brother, who was standing there as if he barely knew her. She hadn't seen him in months, but he hadn't changed much, except maybe for the mustache he was now rocking. He was taller than Jaxon by a couple of inches, with a short curly fade, full lips and bushy eyebrows that she'd always told him needed to get trimmed. He was stylishly dressed in black trousers, a black silk shirt and vest.

The woman at his side was no less as impressive with her distinct African features. She was just as tall as Sean with smooth, flawless dark brown skin and she wore a wisp of a chiffon dress that barely reached her thighs, but on her it looked amazing. It also made Kim feel as if she was an Amazon, instead of a Glamazon like this creature.

She eventually found her voice. "Well, perhaps if you'd help teach me to dance I wouldn't be."

"You've never needed me, Kimmy," Sean replied. "You were born self-sufficient."

Jaxon stepped forward and offered his hand to Sean.

"Jack Scott. Nice to meet you." They shook hands, but Sean didn't bother introducing his date.

"Oh, I'm sorry, Jax—Jack." Kimberly caught herself in time. She knew Jaxon didn't want anyone to know his real identity. "This is my brother Sean Parker."

"Sean." Jaxon nodded as understanding apparently dawned on him.

"It's good to see you," Kimberly said.

"You're looking well," Sean said. "Leadership agrees with you."

Kimberly tried to ignore the dig and attempted to make conversation. "How's the opening of your new restaurant coming along?"

"It's coming."

Her heart sank; he wasn't going to make this easy for her. She stared at Sean for several long moments wishing that he would give her some sign of hope that they could put this distance behind them and move forward, but instead he said, "Our table is ready." He began to walk away, but Kimberly touched his arm.

"Sean, please."

He glanced down at her hand and the scornful stare he gave her as he looked into her eyes told Kimberly he was not interested in healing the wounds between them. He was just as hurt as he'd been six months ago. Time hadn't healed all wounds.

She blinked, trying to hold her tears back. She felt Jaxon's hands at her waist. "Why don't we sit down?" he whispered in her ear.

She nodded as she watched Sean walk away with his date without another word to her. Dazed, Kimberly sat down.

"Are you okay?" Jaxon asked.

"Do you mind if we forego dessert and get out of here?"

"Of course not." He motioned for the waiter and took care of the bill while Kimberly rushed toward the ladies' room.

She didn't want Jaxon to see just how hurt she was by her brother's cold treatment. When she made it to the women's restroom, she leaned against the door and let out a long cry.

Why was Sean being so unreasonable? Why was he treating her as though she'd done him wrong when all she'd done was work hard? She didn't deserve his scorn or his rejection. She walked over to the sink and stared at her reflection. Sadness was in her eyes and that was far from what she'd wanted for this evening. But seeing Sean had caught her off guard. She hadn't been prepared for the depth of his anger toward her. She was beginning to think their relationship was a lost cause.

If it was, she couldn't let it ruin the good thing she had going with Jaxon. They'd been having a good time tonight until she'd seen Sean. She couldn't let it ruin their first official date. She was going to have to put her sibling problem on the shelf and make things right with Jaxon.

When she came out of the ladies' restroom, Jaxon was waiting for her.

"I took care of the check and I got dessert to go." He held up a cardboard box. "I heard their flan is to die for."

Kimberly smiled. "We can eat it later. What else is in store for tonight?"

Jaxon frowned. "I assumed you wanted to get back to the Belleza."

She shook her head. "No, I don't want this evening to end. I'm not going to let anything or anyone ruin our night."

A broad grin spread across Jaxon's face. "I'm glad to hear it." He offered her his arm. "Then let's go."

To lighten the mood, they ended the evening at a nearby casino, where Jaxon supplied Kimberly with an abundance of chips after they'd valet-parked his rented Jaguar.

"I warn you, I don't gamble," Kimberly said as she looked around the casino. "Don't believe in it. Why would people waste good money when the odds are always in the house's favor?"

"Because it can be fun sometimes," Jaxon replied. "Let's try it." He grasped her reluctant hand and pulled her toward the tables.

They started first with the roulette table, then it was on to poker, after which they finally settled on blackjack. Jaxon whispered some tips and his breath was warm and tickled her ear. She nodded her understanding as he explained the general principle of the card game.

"Seems easy enough." She glanced over at him as he took the seat beside her at the table. She decided to bet twenty bucks on her first hand and work up to a larger bet.

The dealer dealt the six players at the table their hand and Kimberly took a peek at her cards. She had an eight and seven. It was a risk, but she was hoping it would pay off. "Hit me."

The dealer gave her another card—a five. Kimberly blew out a sigh of relief. She stayed at twenty. When the dealer busted, she, Jaxon and another player won.

"This is fun!" She smiled at him. Despite what had happened between her and Sean earlier at the restaurant, she was finally starting to relax. Seeing her brother had nearly dashed her hopes for a fun and romantic evening but she was rallying and she didn't want to see the night end.

Kimberly won another three games straight before she increased her bet to fifty-dollar chips.

"You feeling lucky?" Jaxon said.

She caught the intense heat of his gaze. She read his mind and knew what he meant, what would make them both very lucky. The magnitude of their desire for each other was palpable. "Well, that depends on you, doesn't it?"

Jaxon merely smiled and they returned to the game. They played several more hands of blackjack before leaving the table. They were headed to try their hand at another game, when they saw a poster for a burlesque show that evening. It was clear it was somewhat naughty, but also intriguing.

"Should we check it out?" Jaxon asked. He didn't wait for her response; he just pulled her toward the entrance. There was a bouncer at the door, who Jaxon tipped before he opened the rope and let them in.

Kimberly and Jaxon stood near the doorway and watched the show in silence in the dark.

Jaxon was beginning to feel restless, edgy. Watching this show with performers in their skimpy costumes and bustiers was making him extremely horny. He imagined Kimberly wearing one of those outfits. She had just enough bosom to fill out one of those numbers and Jaxon would love to buy her one and have her model it for him.

He could sense Kimberly's uneasiness as she stood beside him. She was much more conservative than he was, so he could only imagine that watching a sexy show like this was out of her comfort zone, but she seemed determined to go with the flow.

When one of the dancers pranced onstage and began to seductively sway her hips, Jaxon couldn't resist the throbbing need in his loins. He pulled Kimberly into a dark corner of the club and kissed her.

His tongue met hers and she angled her head to allow him better access. Their mouths connected, tongues tasted and hands roamed over each other's body in the dark of the nightclub. Blood rushed through his veins and his heart began to beat erratically. Sexual need seeped through him and he could feel his manhood beginning to swell.

He moved his lips from hers long enough to say, "We need to get out of here."

"Yes, we do," she murmured.

They were out of the nightclub and hotel casino and back in the Jaguar in less than five minutes. Once in the car, he wrapped his hand around her neck and drew her to him. He mated his tongue with hers in a French kiss that only hinted at the need that was burning inside him. The kiss was passionate and possessive. If he could, he would give in to his desire now and have Kimberly in the car, but he couldn't. For now, he would take her back to his suite and make love to her until she screamed out his name.

Slowly he pulled away and started the car. "To be continued."

Chapter 12

Once they'd made it to Jaxon's suite, he swept her into his arms and explored her mouth greedily. They didn't bother to turn on the light. Instead they let the moonlight filter in from the drapes and illuminate them. They kicked off their shoes at the doorway and immediately began undressing each other. Jaxon's shirt was the first to go followed by her peplum top and garnet satin plunge bra.

When she was naked from the waist up, Jaxon lifted her in his arms and she wrapped her legs around him as he carried her toward the bedroom.

"We're about to burn up the sheets," Jaxon murmured, seconds before his mouth found her hardened nipple.

She responded with a soft low moan. His actions were like an onslaught against her senses. "Jaxon." She was just as eager to be with him. The ache she'd felt after that kiss in the burlesque club was about to be satisfied as only Jaxon could.

He lowered her onto the bed and then went for the zipper of his trousers and slowly eased them down his long, lean hips. Her gaze rested on his muscular chest before shifting lower to the powerful erection straining in his briefs. She wanted to feel its strength, its power inside her. She sucked in a deep breath when he slid the briefs down his legs and his shaft sprang free. He was big and powerful and she couldn't wait to have him inside her. He walked over to the nightstand and put on a condom before returning to her.

He pulled her toward him at the edge of the bed. She knew what he wanted and helped him by unzipping her jeans. She lifted her hips and in one swift movement, he rid her of the denim along with the thong she'd been wearing. Clearly, he was adept at undressing a woman. Now naked, she reveled in his admiring gaze. He stared at her for long moments, drinking her in, and then crawled on top of her on the bed and took her mouth.

His kiss was demanding and she freely gave herself up to the passion. Her stomach tightened when she felt one of his hands roaming over her rear end as he pulled her firmly to him. His touch wasn't smooth and slow like he usually was; instead he was unabashedly hurried. She could feel the need for him in the center of her legs and, as if Jaxon knew what she needed, he reached between her thighs and stroked her there, first with one finger. Then another. Then another. He had three fingers inside her and was stroking her with deliberate precision. Did he want to decimate her? she wondered. Sensation after sensation began to ripple through her entire body and Kimberly moaned.

"Come for me, baby. Don't hold back." Jaxon moved from her lips to her ear so he could tongue her with fervor.

Kimberly did just that. She didn't hold back; she cried out his name. "Jaxon!"

Contractions were still reverberating through her body when she felt him enter her with a swift thrust, all the while holding her body immobile. She stretched for him and he began moving inside her. Heat flared again inside her. She couldn't think. She just felt.

Jaxon began thrusting, gradually withdrawing and then thrusting deeper again. He seemed to savor each and every one of her gasps as he increased the tempo. She felt raw, unadulterated pleasure of the purest kind and her thighs began to quiver. She climaxed again and this time her release triggered his orgasm and he let out a throaty groan, then collapsed on top of her.

Kimberly sighed as morning light awakened her. Glancing at her watch, she realized she'd missed her morning workout with Gabrielle and Robyn for the second morning in a row. She'd overslept after a night spent making love to Jaxon again. Closing her eyes, she could imagine him lying next to her in her bed, feel him inside her, moving, stroking. Heck, her insides still throbbed from the multiple orgasms he'd given her last night. Too bad she'd left his suite and come back to her condo in the early predawn hours. She wanted him again.

The girls, however, were going to be suspicious of her out-of-character behavior. Instead of imagining more lovemaking with Jaxon, she'd best think of a plausible excuse to give Gabrielle and Robyn. But she ran out of time; she had to get to work.

Robyn and Gabrielle caught up to her when she was leaving her condo an hour later.

"There you are," Gabrielle said. "Where the heck have you been?"

"Yeah, what gives?" Robyn asked. "You've missed two morning workouts and that's unlike you."

"It's nothing. Anyway, I was just about to leave," Kimberly said, attempting to shut her door behind her, but the girls pushed her back inside her condo.

"Oh, no, you don't." Robyn grabbed her by the arm

and closed the door behind her. "You're going to tell us what you've been up to the last two days."

"I—I—I haven't been up to anything," she lied as she pulled away from Robyn and walked into the kitchen. She turned on her Keurig coffeemaker. "I've just been really busy." She opened the upper cabinet and pulled out a K-Cup and a mug. She placed the disc into the machine, pressed the on button and waited for it to brew.

"Is that right?" Gabrielle began circling Kimberly. "Because the concierge told us that Jack Scott asked for suggestions to a fine-dining restaurant and rented a car last night. And the day before yesterday neither of us could reach you all afternoon. Your phone kept going to voice mail, all day *and* all night."

"Spill the beans, Kimberly Parker," Robyn ordered.

"You might as well confess because we are not letting you out of this condo until you do," Gabrielle added.

After her coffee was done, Kimberly reached for the mug and drank it black. She didn't need the extra calories and she needed the added fortification to deal with her pushy friends this morning. "Okay, okay." She threw up her hands in surrender. "Okay. Jax—Jack and I have been spending time together." Good thing she caught herself before she compounded the situation by using his real name with her friends.

"Define 'spending time together.'" Robyn eyed her warily.

Kimberly released a long sigh. There was no way she was going to be able to keep this to herself anymore. She let the cat out of the bag. "We spent the night together, actually the last two nights."

"You did the nasty with Jack?" Gabrielle teased.

"Yes." Kimberly lowered her head in shame, especially considering she was the biggest proponent of the Belleza's rules.

"How was it?" Robyn asked, clearly eager for more juicy details.

Kimberly rolled her eyes. "Wonderful, hot, steamy, amazing. I can't think of enough adjectives to describe this man." She glanced over at Gabrielle as she fanned herself with her hand. "I take it you disapprove."

"I don't disapprove per se as this is the happiest I've seen you in months, but he is a guest, Kimberly, and haven't you always said we should stay clear of guests?"

Kimberly took another sip of coffee. "I have and I think it's a wise practice. Trust me, I recognize I'm being a hypocrite on this issue."

"But you're still going to keep seeing him?" Gabrielle finished.

"Stop riding her," Robyn said. "We were the ones who encouraged her to go talk to him."

"Talk, maybe even date," Gabrielle replied, "not jump into a sexual relationship with the man."

"Can't you lighten up on this, Gabby?" Kimberly asked. "I'm not saying it's the perfect scenario, but Jack was so compassionate last night, especially after I ran into Sean."

"You saw Sean?" Robyn's entire demeanor changed and she seemed a bit on edge.

Kimberly nodded. "And it wasn't a happy family reunion. He pretty much dissed me in front of his high-fashion-model date."

"He had a date?" Robyn asked with a frown.

"Oh, yeah, some beautiful Glamazon," Kimberly replied. "Whom he didn't even bother introducing. And when I tried to reach out to him, he shut me down cold."

"I'm sorry, Kim," Gabrielle replied. "I wish Sean

could get over his anger toward you and your parents so you can heal."

"Doesn't look like that's happening anytime soon."

"But he did talk to you," Robyn said encouragingly. "He could have ignored you entirely."

Kimberly laughed at Robyn's hopeful attitude. "If you want to look at it like that, then yes. But I'm tired of being Sean's whipping boy. If he wants to make amends, he's going to have to take the next step. I'm done."

Robyn nodded. "I'm sure it'll happen, Kim. Sean just needs a little more time. You'll see. He'll come around."

Kimberly squeezed her friend's hand. "Thanks, gal."

"In the meantime, are you going to continue seeing Jack?" Gabrielle inquired. "You know, after you've had good sex, you'll want it on the regular, so it would be hard to go without."

Kimberly laughed at Gabrielle's bluntness. "Yes, I'm going to see him again."

"Just be careful," Robyn advised. "I don't want you to get hurt or too attached when he inevitably leaves."

Robyn was right on that front, thought Kimberly. She had no idea just how long Jaxon was going to stay at the Belleza, but she didn't want to think about that. For now, his stay was open-ended. And as long as he was here, Kimberly intended to take advantage of every minute.

But first she had business to tend to.

When she got to her office and checked her messages, one in particular stood out. From her mother. She was hoping the ice had thawed between her parents. She called her immediately and made a lunch date for that afternoon at The Pearl.

When she walked in, her mother was already seated at a table by the windows that overlooked the main lawn, but rose when she saw Kimberly.

Kimberly had to admit Ilene Parker looked phenomenal. Her reddish-brown hair had been stylishly curled so that it fell in soft layers down her shoulders. The cream suit she wore and matching heels suited her.

"Mom." Kimberly came forward and kissed her mother's cheek.

"Kimberly." Her mother returned her embrace. "It's so good to be back here." She glanced around the dining room. "But it's strange at the same time, knowing I'm no longer running the Belleza with your father."

"I bet. I'm sure I would feel the same." Kimberly took a seat at the table and accepted the menu from the hostess. "How are you, otherwise?" She eyed her mother's smooth brown skin, which barely had a wrinkle.

"I could be better."

"So I take it you and Daddy haven't kissed and made up?" Kimberly inquired.

"Far from it," her mother responded. "He's been sleeping in the guest bedroom the last two nights."

"Mom…" Kimberly sighed as she perused the menu. "You have to end this. You can't let the Belleza come between the two of you."

Her mother placed the menu on the table and stared at Kimberly. "Then your father shouldn't have accused your brother. Sean would never have done what your father accused him of."

"I agree, but isn't there enough strife in our family without adding more fuel to the fire?" Kimberly asked.

When the waitress came, they each placed similar orders of passion-fruit iced tea and salad before returning to the conversation.

"Yes, but I don't know how to make things right," her mother admitted.

"Neither do I." Kimberly reached for her mother's

hand across the table. She gave it a gentle squeeze. "Matter of fact, I called Sean."

"You did?"

Kimberly nodded. "But he didn't pick up."

"Oh, Kimmy," her mother started, but she interrupted her.

"It gets worse. Last night, while out on a date, I ran into Sean."

"A date? Sean?" Her mother shook her head. "I want to hear about each."

"I'll start with Sean. We spoke and he was cordial, but when I reached out to him to heal the rift, I was shot down cold."

"Oh, honey."

Kimberly shrugged. "Trust me, Mom, it hurt. I've never seen Sean look at me like that before. We've always been so close, but last night I couldn't reach him."

"Neither can I." Her mother's eyes welled with tears. "He won't return my calls. He's closed himself off from the entire family except Ryan. At least he returns my calls."

"As much as I hate to say it, we have to let him come around in his own time."

"I suppose you're right," her mother responded. "Who would have thought that the daughter would teach the mother?"

"Oh, I haven't learned everything from you yet."

The waitress came back with their drinks and salad in record time. Given their status, Kimberly wasn't surprised their order had been rushed through, but she hoped not to the detriment of other guests.

"What can I offer you?"

"Hmm…" Kimberly smiled. "Perhaps some words of wisdom on how to deal with my new beau."

"A new beau? Would that be the one you've been 'dating'?"

Kimberly nodded. "Although there's an air of mystery about him, it feels like I've known him for years. And, well, the chemistry between us is spot-on. Have you ever felt that way before, Mama?"

"I have, with your father. The night we first met and to this day I still get a little giddy every time he comes into a room."

"Even when you're upset with him?"

"Even then."

"Aww…" Kimberly felt that way about Jaxon. Every time she saw him she felt butterflies in her stomach and her heart would nearly leap out of her chest. Could her feelings for Jaxon be stronger than she'd imagined?

"I guess I should let your father out of the doghouse, huh?" her mother inquired, breaking into her thoughts.

"I think it's time," Kimberly said with a smile.

Chapter 13

Jaxon was excited to spend another day with Kimberly. It was the weekend and she'd taken the day off so they could spend it together, and he'd planned something romantic.

They'd spent the past few nights together and it had been a slice of heaven. He thought that if he made love to her all week that somehow he would exorcise her out of his system, but it was having the opposite effect. The more time he spent with her, the more he wanted to *be* with her. She had a body that was made for loving. She was slim and trim with just enough curves for him to grab hold of.

"Mr. Scott," the valet interrupted his thoughts while he stood in the lobby. "I've brought the Jaguar around for you."

"Thanks." Jaxon handed him a twenty-dollar bill and walked toward the car. He drove over to Kimberly's condo and she was waiting for him outside by the curb wearing cutoff jean shorts and a skimpy tank top.

He quickly jumped out of the car and came around to open her door. "You ready for a day of fun?"

She held up an oversize knapsack. "Yep."

He helped her inside and minutes later they were headed off-site. Jaxon had a special day planned. First they would hike up the canyon after a short tram ride midway to the top and then have some dinner later. He'd told Kimberly to bring a change of clothes and from the looks of the bag, she'd complied.

"I think I know where we're going," Kimberly said as they began to make their way to the tram station.

Jaxon shrugged. "I thought it might be nice to have some fresh, clean air and do a little hiking. How does that sound?"

"I'm not much of a hiker or outdoorsy person," Kimberly admitted. "So you'll have to bear with me. I prefer to get my workout indoors."

"Be happy to." Jaxon appreciated that she was up to the challenge even though it was out of her comfort zone.

They parked the Jaguar and walked the pebbled path to the station, where they purchased their tickets for the ten-minute aerial tram ride. On board he learned something about her that he wouldn't have guessed.

Once the tram began soaring through the air, Kimberly reached for his hand and clenched it between her damp palms.

"Are you okay?"

She shook her head.

"Why? What is it?" He looked at her in alarm when he saw a bead of sweat forming on her forehead and felt her hold on his hand turning into a death grip.

"I—I'm afraid of heights," she said and immediately turned into his chest and away from the beautiful, serene sight of the mountaintops.

"Baby." He grabbed both sides of her face and peered into her brown eyes. "Why didn't you say something? We could have done something else."

"B-because I didn't want to ruin this for you. You seemed so excited to come up here."

"You don't ever have to hold anything back from me,

Kimberly. Do you hear me? Just be honest and straight with me, always. Promise me that."

She glanced up at him. "I promise." And then she wrapped her arms around his middle, rested her cheek against his chest and gave him a tight squeeze that she maintained until the tram came to a stop.

Once on solid land, Kimberly let out a deep sigh as Jaxon went to the small store to get some cold bottled water. She hadn't realized she'd nearly been holding her breath the last few minutes of the ride. She knew her fear of heights was irrational, but ever since a turbulent flight coming back from her boarding school when she was thirteen, she couldn't shake her paranoia. She'd been too embarrassed to tell Jaxon about it before the tram ride. He thought she was so put together and she hadn't wanted him to see her fear, but he seemed to be okay with it. In fact, he'd helped her through it. She was finding him to be a compassionate, kind man—a man she could easily fall for.

Jaxon returned with the bottled water and put them in their knapsacks. "You ready to head out?"

"Let's do this." Kimberly put on a good front even though the idea of spending the day becoming one with nature was not her idea of a good time.

Fours hours later, it turned out she was wrong. Hiking wasn't as bad as she'd thought. They'd walked slowly through the trails while munching on Gabrielle's homemade trail mix until they reached one of the National Monuments in the park, where they'd read about its history. Then they'd shared a picnic in a small cave set back from the trail.

"How did you find this?" Kimberly asked as Jaxon lent her a hand and helped her up the rocks to the cave.

"Eagle eye," Jaxon said, smiling. He looked around the small cave for any signs of snakes or other creatures as he spread out the blanket he'd brought in his knapsack.

"The view is breathtaking from up here," Kimberly said, surprising herself when she mustered the courage to look out over the canyon. It was as if the mountains went on for miles.

"I know." Jaxon came up behind her and wrapped his arms around her, resting his chin on her shoulder. "Aren't you glad you came?"

She turned to glance behind her. "Yes, I am."

He rewarded her with a scorching kiss that nearly took her breath away. When he released her, he said, "Ready for some lunch?"

"Famished." And she'd come prepared. She'd had Gabrielle pack them some sandwiches, which were bountiful with meat and cheese, along with baked chips and oatmeal-raisin cookies for dessert. It was a simple lunch, but Jaxon hadn't seemed to mind because it filled their bellies while they talked politics and, to Kimberly's surprise, sports. She wasn't much on football or basketball, but she knew her way around a tennis court and she found they shared a love of Venus and Serena Williams.

They even showed each other some war wounds. Jaxon had had a rotator cuff injury and showed her the scar on his shoulder, and Kimberly pointed to some faint scars on her knee from crashing onto the court as she'd lunged for a ball when she'd played junior varsity tennis.

She followed Jaxon's gaze from the scars to the hem of her shorts and higher. She blushed and her heart began beating faster.

"Slide over this way," he whispered.

The atmosphere between them suddenly became charged with tension. Sexual tension. "Why?"

"Because you're too far away." The hungry look in his eyes told her that when she did, they wouldn't be *talking* anymore.

She complied and he reached out and pulled her into his lap. That was when she felt his erection protruding through his shorts. He'd gotten aroused just by talking to her? Did she really have that kind of power over him?

He laid his head against her chest and his tongue flicked out to lick her nipples through her tank top. "Mmm..." she moaned as she felt his hands at her back.

"Does this thing have a combination lock?" Jaxon asked, trying to unlatch her bra.

"Jaxon!" Kimberly grabbed his head to stop him even though the place between her legs had begun to throb. "What are you doing? What if someone sees us?"

"No one will." Jaxon smiled when the latch on her bra finally gave way and he could caress her nipples freely without interference. "The cave is away from the trail."

"But—but what if they do?" She stuttered her words as he massaged her breasts under her tank top.

"Then they'll get a quite a show." He shocked her when he swiftly lifted the tank top over her head. She was powerless to stop him because she could feel her breasts literally ache for his mouth. So when his mouth closed over one pebble and sucked hard, Kimberly could only sigh. He seemed to know exactly what she needed, what she wanted at any given moment.

She moaned even louder, but did manage to ask, "What about protection?"

Jaxon reached into his pocket and pulled out a three-pack of condoms.

"And you just happen to have those handy?"

"I always carry them now," he admitted with a sly

grin. "Never know when the time to be spontaneous might arise."

"I don't know…" Kimberly was already naked from the waist up, but she was leery of getting caught completely naked and arrested for indecent exposure by some park ranger.

"C'mon, live dangerously." Jaxon moved upward from her breasts. He placed tiny kisses along her neck before going higher to tease her earlobe with his hot, wet tongue. He knew that was her weak spot. "You know you want to," he whispered as his hands began roaming to her shorts. She could feel him unbuttoning the top button, could feel him unzipping them, could feel the gentle caress of his hands as they pushed past her panties and made their way to her moistness.

His finger parted her slick folds so he could tease her feminine core. He used his skillful fingers to make her entire body tremble with need. He stroked her with expert precision and had her writhing with passion in his lap.

"Do you know just how much your scent is arousing me?" Jaxon murmured, flicking his tongue faster and faster inside her ear. "How much it turns me on?"

Kimberly could only shake her head as he assaulted her with relentless strokes of his tongue and fingers. Unconsciously her hips began to undulate against him. "Jaxon, please."

"Please what?"

Kimberly was embarrassed that he could make her want him so blatantly and publicly, but the need to have him was so strong. "I need you inside me!"

"Gladly." Jaxon quickly pulled his hands out of her shorts.

Before she could react, he had her flat on her back on the blanket as he pulled her shorts and thong down her

legs. She looked up at him and watched his quick movement as he unzipped his shorts and pushed them down to
his ankles. He didn't even bother to take them off; he just
slid on a condom, spread her legs wide and entered her.

"Jaxon!" Kimberly rose slightly off the blanket from
the impact of having him inside her. The pleasure was
so intense she thought she might die from it, but Jaxon
wouldn't let her. Each time he surged forward, her body
expanded to take all of him, and when he retreated, she
couldn't wait for him to return.

"You are so damn sexy that I'm addicted to you,"
Jaxon said as he pumped inside her with deliberate precision.

"And I you."

She was milking him, thought Jaxon as she squeezed
her pelvis against him. Milking him of everything that
he had. Making him delirious with a need for her he
couldn't explain. She was stirring things inside him and
becoming his weakness.

He could feel her breath quickening as he thrust in and
out, in and out. He knew convincing her to make love in
the cave was completely out of character, but he didn't
care. He had to have her *now.* Yet, he wanted to make
it special for her, so he yielded control, bringing her up
astride him in her favorite position.

"Ride me, baby. Ride me."

Kimberly did as she was told and grabbed ahold of
his shoulders and took charge. "I like riding." She kissed
him greedily and he released a sharp intake of breath.

He gripped her hips and said, "Go for it!"

She pressed her knees into his thighs and bounced
atop of him. She kept going, vigorously, never letting

up. "Kimberly, baby, you have no idea what you're doing to me."

"I do know. C-cause you're doing the same to me." She looked at him and he looked at her. The knowledge that they were out in the open only added to the allure and the excitement. Then she changed course and slowly began rocking against him, undulating her hips and turning him on even more. He could feel her inner muscles tightening and the rapturous look on her face told him her orgasm was coming.

The next time she came down on him, Jaxon couldn't take any more. He raised his lower body to meet hers and this time they both exploded simultaneously. He gripped her hips and pulled her head down to meet his waiting mouth and got lost in her kiss.

Chapter 14

Kimberly couldn't believe what had just happened between her and Jaxon. She'd made love to him in public, where anyone walking by could have seen them going at it like rabbits! She'd never done anything like that in her entire life. How did he make her do things she'd never done before?

She'd lost all rational thought and had given in to her base desires. But that wasn't all. Something had changed when they'd made love in that cave, or at least it had for Kimberly. She'd really looked at him as they'd made love and she'd gotten swept away in emotion. She was developing strong feelings for him when she was supposed to remain unemotional.

Jaxon wasn't offering her a commitment of any kind. He was only offering her right now while he was estranged from his family. What happened to them afterward when his family kissed and made up? Kimberly had no idea. She was trying her best not to think about it, but it was impossible not to. Jaxon was beginning to mean more to her than she ever could have imagined.

Jaxon Dunham wasn't the only one on her mind right now as she sat at her desk reviewing her calendar. It had been a week since she'd last heard from his sister, Hayley, and she was eager to know if the Dunham Foundation had made a decision on whether they would be holding their event at the Belleza. Could she ask Jaxon? She could, but she didn't want business to interfere in their relationship no matter how important this event was to the resort. She would just have to wait and see.

Tired of the office, Kimberly decided to complete one of her weekly thorough property inspections. She slipped on a white blazer over her sleeveless navy shirt dress with a skinny belt, grabbed her clipboard and headed toward the door.

"I'll be back in a couple of hours," she advised her assistant and grabbed the keys to the golf cart off the hook by the door.

She started at the entrance to the property, where a guest's first experience with the Belleza began. She found the sod in good shape, but several of the Loropetalum and Indian Hawthorn along the driveway needed pruning. The Asiatic Jasmine needed some additional plants to fill it in as ground cover. She made a note to contact her landscaper. The pavement was in good shape after they'd resealed the grounds last year, so she found no issues. She parked the golf cart near the side of the lobby valet area so as to not interfere with guests on their arrival.

The valet immediately greeted her as he should, as did the bellboy and front-desk clerk. "Good morning," she said as she nodded to her staff. She noted that the marble was looking well polished, all the light fixtures were working overhead and the flowers on the front table were appropriately arranged and blooming. She was grateful for her staff that paid attention to the details.

She continued her inspection of the lobby and made her way toward the Plaza. There guests meandered down

the pebbled path, while small boutiques offered everything from clothes to jewelry.

Eventually she made her way to the Ruby Retreat, the
Belleza's bar and lounge, where she found Jonah wiping
glasses as the janitorial staff steam-cleaned the red up-
holstered furniture and the carpet.

She smiled when she saw him. "Jonah." He had on
his usual tuxedo shirt with bow tie and plaid vest. She
wondered how many such outfits Jonah had in his closet.

"Hey there, pretty lady," he said when he saw her.
"Where have you been hiding yourself these days?"

"Hi, Jonah," she said, taking a seat on a stool at the bar.
She'd missed seeing the elderly gentleman who wasn't
just an employee but an old family friend, but her focus
had been elsewhere thanks to a certain handsome guest.

"You've been MIA of late," Jonah said. "Haven't seen
you come in with the girls this week."

"Yeah, I've been pretty busy," Kimberly responded
with a sly grin.

"Is that right? I bet I know why you've been walking
around with a smile on your face."

Kimberly stared back at him. "You do?"

He nodded as he put away the glasses he'd cleaned.
"I've got ears and eyes, and I can tell when a man has
caught your eye. You haven't been this happy in…well,
a long time."

She couldn't help but smile. Jonah was as sly as a fox
and very observant. "You think you know me so well?"

"Girl." He slapped the bar with the towel that he'd been
using. "I've known you since you were in a diapers. Hell,
before then, when you were just in your mama's belly."

Kimberly couldn't help but chuckle at Jonah's forth-
rightness. Trust him to keep it real at his age. There was
no time to beat around the bush.

"I'm just glad to see it," Jonah said.

"See what?'

"You in such good spirits. It's high time you found yourself a fella and stopped moping because that knuckle-headed brother of yours refuses to see the truth."

"Which is?"

"That you were clearly more suited and more capable of running the Belleza than he could ever be." When Kimberly began to protest, Jonah held up his hand. "That's not to say that Sean isn't a gifted chef, but that doesn't mean he's fit to run a place like this." Jonah motioned around the bar. "You just have to continue on this path you're going down."

"Who says I was going to stop?"

Jonah cocked his head and stared boldly at her. "You have to keep your heart open, Kimmy, and it seems like you're finally doing that. Keep on. Don't lose sight of what's important."

"Do you have regrets, Jonah?" Kimberly asked. She'd never thought the lifelong bachelor had any, but his advice certainly made her wonder if he did.

"You don't know everything about me, Kim. I've lived much longer than you have. And what I'm saying is that life is too short and one day you don't want to look back and regret letting a good man like Jack Scott get away."

Kimberly frowned. "Who says I'm seeing Jack Scott?"

He snatched off his eyeglasses and handed them to her. "I'm blind without them, but when I've got them on, I've got twenty-twenty." He motioned from his eyes to hers as if he could see her.

"I thought I was doing a good job of hiding it." She handed Jonah back his glasses, which he promptly put back on. "I wouldn't want any of the staff to find out."

"And they won't," Jonah responded. "I sort of eavesdropped the other day and caught Robyn and Gabrielle debating the issue."

Kimberly rolled her eyes. Had anyone else heard them? She didn't want to be called out by her staff for inappropriate behavior

"Don't go getting all mad at them, ya hear?" Jonah said as he came around the bar toward her. "They're your family and they only want what's best for you. Like I do."

"I know, Jonah. And I promise to keep an open mind—" she glanced around her to make sure no one was listening "—when it comes to you know who."

"That's all I can ask for." He wrapped her in his arms for one of his special Jonah bear hugs.

Kimberly had the evening to herself so she and the girls were going to a wine bar for a little girls' time and catch-up. She really hadn't seen them much in the past two weeks since most of her evenings and even her mornings were now tied up with Jaxon.

"I can't believe we actually get to hang out with you tonight," Gabrielle replied when they arrived at the wine room. "I thought we were going to have to uncuff you from the bed that Jack has you tied to."

"I haven't been that bad," Kimberly said as she handed the cashier her card and a fifty-dollar bill to load to it so she could sample the fifty or more wine selections.

"You wanna bet?" Robyn asked. "You haven't made it to our morning workout in weeks."

"She's been getting a workout of the penile variety," Gabrielle replied.

And they all began laughing uncontrollably. "You're shameless!" Kimberly blushed.

After they'd settled on some selections, a Merlot for Kimberly, a Cabernet Sauvignon for Gabrielle and a sweet Moscato for Robyn, they sat down on the plush leather sofas strategically placed around the wine pourers and cabinets lined with bottles.

"So catch us up," Robyn asked. "What don't we know?"

Kimberly laughed and prepared for a serious dish session. She told them about their talks, but the highlight was their hike to the canyon.

"You went hiking?" Robyn replied, "You hate exercising in the elements."

"Yes, I do," Kimberly said, placing her wineglass on the cocktail table. "But I didn't want to disappoint him. He really wanted to ride the tram to the top."

"But you're deathly afraid of heights," Gabrielle added.

"Which is why his hand was just about broken when we made it to the top."

"You really need to get over your fear of heights," Robyn replied. "How do you think we're going to make it to Paris and cross it off your bucket list?"

"Swim." Gabrielle laughed. Kimberly rolled her eyes at her, but she merely shrugged and reached for her wineglass that she'd sat on the table and took a generous sip.

"Well, I conquered my fear and made it to the top and we went hiking and—" She paused when she saw Trina Erickson.

"Oh, Lord, here comes trouble," Gabrielle said as she followed the direction of Kimberly's gaze.

Three pairs of eyes landed on Trina. They all knew Trina from boarding school, and they equally despised her. She was a beautiful woman with a medium brown complexion, long dark straight hair and a tall, stunning figure, especially in the Dior pantsuit she was wearing. But she was a spoiled brat. Ever since boarding school, Trina had lorded her wealth over all of them. She'd been born into privilege much like Gabrielle and looked down on anyone who wasn't.

Kimberly's parents had earned their wealth and Trina had always made a point to remind her of her working-class parents, while she'd bullied poor Robyn, who'd come from the projects in New York City. But Robyn had been no punk. She and Trina had gone toe-to-toe several times, until eventually Gabrielle and Kimberly had stepped in. They'd taken Robyn under their wing and after a few months at Merriweather, no one could tell Robyn apart from their rich classmates.

They'd all come to hold Trina in the same regard as a pebble on the bottom of their shoe, one they had to deal with. It hadn't helped that Trina had dated Sean briefly when her parents had taken an extended stay at the Belleza. Kimberly had always believed that Trina had done it on purpose, convincing her parents to choose the Belleza so Kimberly's family could wait on them hand and foot. Dating Sean had added insult to injury, but thankfully, it hadn't lasted long. Sean had realized there wasn't much underneath the beauty and had given Trina her walking papers.

"If it isn't the three musketeers," Trina scoffed when she made it to their table. "How's working life treating you?"

Kimberly rolled her eyes at the reminder that Trina didn't have to work like they did. "Just fine, Trina. How are you?"

"I'm fabulous as always." Trina tossed her silky black hair over her shoulder as she surveyed the three of them sitting on the sofa. "I'm actually glad I ran into you."

"Wish I could say the same," Robyn said underneath her breath.

"What was that?" Trina leaned over and gave Kimberly an unwanted view of her cleavage in the deep V of the pantsuit jacket she wore.

"Oh, nothing," Robyn said. "What can we do for you, Trina? We're in the middle of something here."

Trina narrowed her eyes. "Well, I wouldn't want to intrude, so I'll get right to the point. My birthday is coming up soon and I'm considering having my big blowout party at the Belleza. That's if you could handle a party of this scale and with my class of people."

Kimberly held back Robyn's arm. She knew her friend would love to strangle the woman.

"I mean you have heard a new hotel is opening? The Pinnacle, I believe it's called? I hear it's going to be modern and top-of-the-line. Apparently, no expense has been spared."

"We've heard," Kimberly replied. "But they don't have our long-standing reputation in the community."

"Or me as executive chef," Gabrielle added confidently.

"They might be happy about that considering some of the bad reviews the Belleza has had recently," Trina responded tartly. "I just thought I might help you by giving you some business, considering we're old friends."

"That's really kind of you, Trina," Robyn said. "Why don't you arrange an appointment with my assistant and we'll chat about your upcoming birthday?"

"Sounds great! I'll let you get back to whatever important topic you were discussing." Trina gave them a fake wave before sauntering off with her posse of friends waiting for her at the cheese bar.

"Can you believe that cow?" Robyn asked. "Acting as if she would be doing us a favor if she brought her event to the Belleza."

"Why do you let her get under your skin?" Kimberly asked. "She's not worth it."

"You're telling me her throwing shade on us doesn't bother you?" Gabrielle asked. "'Cause I would beg to differ. I seem to remember that when she was dating Sean you wouldn't have minded ringing that hussy's neck."

Kimberly couldn't help but chuckle. "You're right. She does rub me the wrong way, but I'm in much too good of a headspace to have Trina of all people ruin it."

"Ah, yes, that brings us back to you and Jack," Gabrielle said. "You had just left off at the part where you went hiking and…"

"And…" Kimberly glanced around, then motioned the girls closer to form a tight circle. "Then we made love in a cave."

"You did what?" Robyn asked, pushing away from the circle.

"I know." Kimberly giggled like a schoolgirl. "It was completely out of character, but I just got carried away in the moment."

"In public?" Gabrielle's eyes were as large as saucers. "You little freak! This man certainly has you wrapped around his little finger. You must have strong feelings for him."

"I like him."

Gabrielle and Robyn gave her dubious looks.

"Like?" Gabrielle was the first one to speak. "Oh, no, it's more than that, because having sex in public is something *I* would do, not you."

Robyn nodded. "So, did you enjoy your tryst in the woods?"

"Immensely." Kimberly smiled from ear to ear.

"I'm glad to hear it," Robyn said. "But you have to be careful. I don't want you to get hurt. I mean what do you really know about Jack, other than the fact that he's been staying at the Belleza for weeks? I mean he has to leave eventually. What then?"

Kimberly frowned. "Enough with the questions, Robyn. I thought you wanted me to date. Now that I am, you're raining on my parade?"

"I'm not raining on it," Robyn said. "I'm just leery and a little suspicious of a man who's spent so much of his time at the resort without getting back to his everyday life. We want you to have fun, but be cautious with your heart."

It was too late, Kimberly thought, because they were right to be worried. She had fallen in love with Jaxon, but he only thought of her as a momentary pleasure. Now what was she going to do?

Chapter 15

Jaxon had a war going on inside him. Enough time had passed, nearly six weeks, since the engagement debacle for him to feel guilty about staying away so long from his family, but he was having a hard time even thinking about leaving the Belleza because in the past three weeks he'd gotten to know Kimberly. He didn't know how it happened, but his strong attraction to her had shocked the hell out of him. They'd spent every night together for weeks and he hadn't so much as come up for air. Hadn't wanted to. Which was why he'd had to leave Belleza for the evening. He needed to get some perspective.

He'd driven nearly two hours to a suburb of Los Angeles to meet up with Nate. Nate was a happily married man with a wife and two beautiful children, a boy and a girl, but he'd been only too happy to come out for the evening for a break from domestic bliss.

"It's good to see you, Jack," Nate Griffin said when Jaxon walked into the sports bar.

Nate was an affable fellow with a medium build and a short crew cut, which he'd kept the same length since serving seven years in the navy. He was dressed comfortably in jeans and a deep lavender T-shirt that blended well with his dark chocolate skin.

Jaxon returned his brotherly hug before sitting beside him at the bar. "Good to see you, too."

"So what have you been up to the last couple of months since your parents and Stephanie blew up your world?" Nate asked, reaching for the spicy peanuts on the bar and throwing a few into his mouth.

"Had to get out of Dodge," Jaxon replied. "Until the heat died down, ya know."

"I hear you," Nate said. "But you've been gone for a while. When are you coming back?"

"That's the thing," Jaxon said. "I don't know."

The bartender came up to them and asked, "What can I get you?"

"A Bud Light, same as him." Jaxon inclined his head to the bottle sitting in front of Nate.

"Be right up," the bartender said.

Nate swiveled around in his bar stool. "Let me guess, a female?"

Jaxon frowned. "How did you know?"

"What always trips up men?" Nate replied. "Women. You remember how I was when I first met Audrey. I was a besotted fool. And now that you mention it…" He glanced at Jaxon up and down. "I think I see some of it on you. Or," he said, leaning into Jaxon, "should I say, I smell it?"

Jaxon gave Nate a gentle shove. "Shut the heck up."

"Am I right? Or am I right?"

Jaxon rolled his eyes and was silent before finally responding, "You're right."

"What's her name?" Nate took a swig of his beer.

"Kimberly Parker."

"How'd you guys meet?"

"She owns the resort where I'm staying." The bartender slid a bottle of beer across the bar toward Jaxon. "Thanks." He took a long pull.

"Which is?" Nate queried.

"As much as I love you, man, I'm keeping that one to myself. Walls have ears and I don't want it to get back to my family."

"Must be close by if you could meet me tonight," Nate responded.

Jaxon shrugged and took another swallow of beer.

"So what's the problem?"

"The problem is I wasn't looking," Jaxon replied. "I went there to get away from a woman, not find a new one. And now she's got me twisted."

"Twisted in a good way or a bad way?" Nate asked. When Jaxon stared at him in bewilderment, he continued, "It's a valid question. Twisted could go either way."

Jaxon laughed. "I suppose you're right. To answer your question, twisted in a good way. I'm addicted to her." He downed the last of his beer, which he realized he'd drunk rather fast. Was he really that nervous about the conversation topic?

"*Addicted* is a strong word."

Jaxon turned to his friend. "But true, I mean I've never had such a strong physical response to a woman before. If it was up to me, I'd have her on her back 24/7."

Nate laughed. "You are twisted. Hey, barkeep. Get this man another bottle." He pointed to Jaxon's empty bottle of Bud.

"I was hoping that after a couple of weeks, the attraction would subside, you know? And I would just move on with my life and come back to LA. I mean, I haven't made her any promises."

"But?"

"But what?" Jaxon asked, glancing sideways at him. "I live in Beverly Hills. She lives—well, she lives there and I'm just not interested in settling down, never have been."

"But you could see yourself with this girl?" Nate asked. "Can't you?"

Jaxon glared at him. Why was it that Nate could understand what he was having a hard time wrapping his mind around? "I don't know. Maybe."

"It's got you running scared, right?" Nate asked. "Trust me, I understand. But when you know, you know. Don't fight it, because it'll only bring you both a world of hurt. Just let the relationship take its natural course, in its own way."

Jaxon nodded. It was good advice and he was going to try to take it. "Thanks, man." He clicked his bottle against Nate's.

Even though she had her usual morning workout and breakfast with the girls by the pool, something in Kimberly was off. She tried to tell herself she didn't know why, but she did. She was out of sorts because she'd slept alone last night. Jaxon had gone to spend some time with a friend in Los Angeles and she'd slept fitfully without him.

In a short time, she'd gotten used to having him beside her in the bed. She loved spooning and cuddling her bottom against him. It made her feel safe and secure. But last night she'd missed it, craved it, which was why she hadn't gotten much sleep and was cranky today. She'd snapped at her assistant earlier that morning and had to apologize for her sour disposition. She was hoping the fresh air as she walked the grounds during her weekly inspection would make her feel better.

Instead, it had the opposite effect. No sooner than she was on the golf cart and driving the property that she heard sirens. She followed the sound and watched in hor-

ror as two fire trucks came barreling down the driveway.
She watched them head toward the Plaza.

"Oh, God!" She pushed on the accelerator and rushed
to follow them. By the time she reached them, firemen
were putting out a fire in the Ruby Retreat.

Jonah was standing in the Plaza looking stunned and
out of sorts.

Kimberly rushed toward the older man. "Jonah, are
you okay?" She searched his face and then began patting
his chest and arms for any sign of injury.

"I'm fine, I'm fine, Kimmy." He swatted her hands
away. "Though I can't say the same about the Ruby Retreat." He looked toward the lounge.

"What's going on?" Kimberly asked.

"I don't know," Jonah answered. "One minute I'm
going to storage to stock up the bar and the next minute
a fire. Don't know how something like this could have
happened."

"Neither do I."

A half hour later, the fire was put out and the fire chief
came over to Jonah and Kimberly, who was hanging up
the line with the Belleza's insurance carrier. "Which one
of you is in charge?" he asked.

Kimberly nodded. "I am. I'm the general manager.
Jonah, why don't you get checked out?" She inclined her
head toward the exit. "Make sure you don't have smoke
inhalation or something."

"That's not necessary, Kim." He balked, but she was
having none of it.

"I agree," the fire chief beside her replied. "My men
will take care of you." He motioned one of his crew over
and they led Jonah away, much to his consternation.

Kimberly turned to the fire chief. "Can you tell me
what started the fire?"

"Looks like a cigarette was left unattended."

"A cigarette?" Kimberly was perplexed. "The Belleza is a no-smoking facility."

"Then you might want to remind your guests," he responded. "Because this," he replied as he held up the ashtray with an incinerated cigarette butt, "was definitely the cause."

Kimberly nodded. "I will and thank you for putting out the fire."

"It was a pretty small fire that was contained to the lounge area, but you'll want to get your insurance adjuster in there right away."

"Sure thing," Kimberly said. She shook his hand and watched as he and the other men grabbed their hoses and other equipment and headed toward the exit.

Kimberly stared back at the lounge. She would have to go in and assess the damage, but first she had to deal with her staff and the onlookers standing around. She even heard someone mention the curse of the Belleza. Oh, Lord, that was all she needed. Folks talking about ancient history. "All right, folks, the show is over. Everything's okay and the fire has been put out. You can go on to your other activities."

"What happened?"

"How could this have started?" Several of the Belleza staff came toward her and started firing questions.

Kimberly glanced around at the guests who were still watching them. "We'll talk about this at tomorrow's meeting. In the interim, let's get back to work." She clapped her hands to get the staff and guests moving.

Eventually the crowd began to disperse, but she still heard whispers about the Belleza curse. She had some serious damage control to do. She began disseminating orders to the staff to cordon off the Ruby Retreat until the insurance adjuster could make a site visit and repairs could be made.

She was just finishing up when she saw Jaxon jogging toward her on the pebbled path. She couldn't stop herself; her heart skipped a beat. He was a darn good-looking man and she was head over heels for him.

"Is everything okay? Are you okay?" Jaxon asked, nowhere near out of breath as he grasped both sides of her face and surveyed her. "I just pulled into the valet and heard everyone talking about a fire at the lounge and ran over."

"I'm okay," Kimberly said.

"Are you sure about that?" Jaxon rubbed a smudge of fire soot off her face. Worry was written all over her face.

She smiled up at him. "Thank you and yes. It was a small fire. Doesn't look like the Ruby Retreat is damaged too badly. We caught it in time."

"What happened?"

"Let's walk and talk." She grasped one of his biceps and walked him back toward the front entrance. Once they made it to her golf cart, she said, "Hop in."

Jaxon slid in beside her and she kicked the cart into gear and then finally answered his question. "The fire chief said a cigarette was left burning, but here's the thing, Jaxon. The Belleza is a no-smoking facility. So there's no way one of the guests did it, which leads me to believe it was intentional."

"You mean arson?"

"It sounds crazy and I'm sure everyone will think a guest tried to sneak one in, but…" Kimberly trailed off and shook her head. "I have a funny feeling about this."

"Then you should listen to your gut."

"I will," Kimberly replied, "but first I have to squash these curse rumors."

"What curse rumors?"

"You mean you haven't heard?" Kimberly queried, making the turn into his villa. She would have thought that since Jaxon had been staying at the Belleza for as long as he had that someone surely must have told him.

"No, I haven't. Explain."

"There has been a rumor going around for as long as I can remember that the Belleza is cursed." She noted Jaxon's grin, but continued, "The tale dates back to the hotel's beginnings as the Belleza Inn. Back then, there was talk about a buried treasure on the premises. People used to come from all over hoping they could unearth it, but nothing was ever found. Then when my grandparents fell on some hard times and the hotel had some issues, the rumors of a curse began. The theory was that anytime someone got close to discovering the treasure, something bad would happen to them."

"And now you think the rumors will surface again?"

"I don't think—they already have. I heard several staffers and guests talking about it," Kimberly said. "And it's ridiculous. There is no curse. But I do think that someone is out to get us. Why? I don't know, but my gut is telling me that this doesn't add up."

When they stopped, Kimberly prepared to jump out of the cart, but Jaxon stopped her. "Then I need you and the girls to be extra careful. If someone has it out for the Belleza, the three of you are the face of the resort and you may be a target."

"I will." She leaned over and placed a long, lingering kiss across his lips. "I have a few things to deal with thanks to this fire, but I'll see you later tonight."

"Later it is." Jaxon jumped out of the cart. "And I promise I'll help relieve some of your stress."

"Sounds marvelous."

When she made it back to her office there were nearly half a dozen messages for her, but she had something else to take care of. She closed the door behind her and headed to her phone.

Her fingers dialed the number to the private investigator. "Hi, it's Kimberly Parker," she said. "Another incident has occurred. I need you to ramp up your investigation."

A couple of hours later, Jaxon had the mood all set in his suite. He'd contacted the spa and had a massage bed and the essential oils brought up to his suite. At first they'd thought he wanted a massage for himself, but he had other ideas for the night. He intended to give Kimberly one of his personal massages. After her exhausting day it would make her feel better.

He had a lot of time to think after hanging out with Nate last night. They'd both had one too many and had taken a cab back to Nate's. Audrey hadn't been too happy to see two grown men wasted, but she'd put Jaxon up in the guest room, while Nate, poor thing, got the couch. Jaxon had lain awake thinking about Nate's advice and although he hadn't made any promises to Kimberly, he knew he would want to continue seeing her even after he left the Belleza. What that might mean he wasn't sure. He would just have to take things one day at a time.

Kimberly arrived on his doorstep at nearly eight o'clock, an hour after their designated time. "I'm sorry I'm late." She held up a bottle of Merlot. "But I brought an apology gift."

He leaned down and brushed his lips across hers. "I'll take it. C'mon in." He swatted her behind as she entered.

Kimberly, however, stopped short when she saw the

massage bed in the middle of the room. "Um?" She turned to him. "What's going on?"

He took the bottle from her and walked over to the kitchen while she remained in place. "That's for you," he said as searched for a corkscrew. After he uncorked the wine and poured each of them a glass, he walked it over to her. "I'm giving you a massage tonight."

"You are?"

He heard the surprise in her voice. "Yes, I've been told I'm pretty good with my hands." His eyes never left her face and Kimberly blushed at the double entrendre. He knew she had to be remembering the times he'd used his fingers to bring her to one satisfying climax after another.

"That would be accurate," Kimberly said.

Jaxon smiled broadly. "Good, so get naked."

"Excuse me?"

"I need to be able to fully massage you," he responded, "and I can't fully massage you with your clothes on."

"Can I have a few more sips of my wine first?"

"Absolutely." He walked over to the armchair and sat down. "But then I want you naked between the sheets."

She took a few more sips before placing the glass on the nearby side table and began undressing. Jaxon didn't leave the room or turn away; he watched her. He noticed she seemed a little shy at having him staring at her as she undressed, but then she lifted her top over her long, luscious black hair and Jaxon noted that she wasn't wearing a bra.

She caught his appreciative smile and blushed, even though her nipples tightened to little pebbles. Jaxon licked his lips as he imagined what his mouth would like to do to those nipples. He thought about how he would kiss each one, licking and flicking them back and forth between his tongue and teeth until she began to moan. He loved hearing her moan when she liked what he was doing to her. She was very responsive and it was one hell of a turn-on.

Next, she sliding the formfitting yoga pants down her slender hips and Jaxon swallowed when he saw the tiny swatch of lace fabric that covered her feminine mound. He remembered how she smelled in that cave when he'd brought her to an orgasm. How her scent had filled the cave, driving him mad and making him pound into her without thought to their surroundings. He'd been completely primitive with her and she'd responded to him with equal fervor.

"Jaxon?"

"Hmm…"

"I'm underneath the sheets."

Jaxon blinked. Had he been in a daze and missed her taking off her panties? Damn!

He rose from the armchair and came over to her on the massage table. She was lying facedown with her head in the headrest. "Are you comfortable?" He asked, rubbing her back over the sheets. He admitted he was trying to relax her, but also seeing if she'd been bold enough to take it all off for him.

He got his answer when his hands roamed to her lower back and found no resistance. He smiled knowingly. He was turning Miss Kimberly Parker into an exhibitionist.

"Yes, I'm comfortable."

"Good." He tugged the sheet down to her lower back and walked over to the essential-oils basket. He chose the lavender scent and came back to the table. "Is lavender okay?"

"Hmm…it's fine."

He drizzled some of the lavender-infused oil down her back and then used his hands to massage the oil into her skin. Her skin was soft and supple and Jaxon had to remind himself that he was giving her a massage to help relax *her*, not turn himself on.

Eventually, he found his pace, starting with her shoulders and back, kneading them with long and soft strokes as he'd felt the therapist do to him. Then he moved to her lower back and made circular motions with his hands.

"Oh God, right there," Kimberly moaned.

He continued his ministrations and heard her deep sigh. He'd heard that sitting too long could cause some stress in the lower back and paid special attention to that area. Eventually, he pulled the sheet back to cover her shoulders before uncovering one thigh and leg. He massaged her calves and feet and moved higher to her thighs. He could feel the heat emanating from her core and his touch changed from a message to a caress, so he moved down to her feet, rolling his knuckles back and forth over them. He used the same technique on her other leg and thigh before coming back to her neck and shoulders to massage them a little further.

When he was done, he bent down and whispered in her ear, "How did that feel?"

"Good…"

He noticed her voice had a slight hesitancy to it. "Was I too strong, not strong enough?"

"No, that's not it."

"What then?"

Kimberly rose from the massage table lifting the sheet with her to cover her bosom. "Well…" She paused as if uncomfortable. "I—I thought when you were massaging my thighs, the way you touched me, that…"

"That we were going to make love?"

She blushed. "Yes."

"Trust me, Kimberly, I wanted to, but I also want you to know that this was just a little treat for you. I didn't do it expecting anything in return. I enjoy spending time with you and it doesn't always have to be about sex between us, although I do find we connect very well in that department."

She smiled and lowered her head. "What are we going to do now?"

"How about we watch a movie? I have dinner in the oven from The Pearl."

"That sounds wonderful. I'll get dressed."

Jaxon watched Kimberly slip back into her clothes. He didn't know how he'd restrained himself from taking her on that massage table when every part of him wanted to take her right then and there. He wanted Kimberly to know that she meant more to him that just a bedmate. It was unusual for him to care so much, but then again, Kimberly was one in a million.

Chapter 16

She didn't make her morning workout with the girls because she'd slept in. After Jaxon had given her a massage last night, they'd sat on the sofa watching an action flick and eating dinner. She'd fully expected that after he'd massaged her they'd end the evening in bed as they had every other night, but he'd surprised when he'd told her he wasn't just interested in her as a bedmate.

It warmed her heart to know that he enjoyed spending time with her. On the other hand, as happy as she was, she didn't know what it all meant. Although he'd been completely attentive to her and had made her feel special, he'd never once talked about a future between them, not last night and not ever. Was she deluding herself that he was starting to share the same feelings she had?

She couldn't help but think of Jaxon's ex, Stephanie. Perhaps there was more to the story than what Jaxon had shared with her. Stephanie could have had a legitimate gripe for wanting more or thinking they could have had more if Jaxon behaved with her as he had been with Kimberly. She could see how the woman could have had hope for a future.

All of this was running through her mind when she found the girls sitting out by the pool having quiche lorraine and black coffee.

"May I join you?" she asked when she made it to the table.

"That depends," Robyn said, putting down her fork. "Because you may not like to hear what we have to say."

Kimberly frowned. "What are you talking about?"

Gabrielle pushed a section of newspaper toward her. Kimberly picked it up and scanned the pages. There in black-and-white in the society pages of the *Beverly Hills Times* was yet another headline about Jaxon Dunham and Stephanie Sawyer, along with their photos. It was the first time Kimberly had seen a picture of Stephanie. She could have gone online and searched for information about the woman, but she hadn't wanted anything to sully what Jaxon had told her. But now with the newspaper right in front of her, she couldn't resist taking a seat and skimming the article. Stephanie refused to let her relationship with Jaxon end quietly even though it had been nearly two months since their breakup.

"Where is the elusive bachelor who broke the socialite's heart?" the paper asked. "Is he as heartless as she claims?"

She threw the newspaper down on the table and glanced at her friends. "So you know who he is." She said it more like a statement than a question.

"Yeah," Gabrielle said sarcastically. "Jaxon Dunham of the Dunham Foundation. Kim, how could you keep something like this from us?"

Before she could answer, Robyn asked her, "Did you read that article?" She pointed to the society section she'd thrown back on the table. "It says that he led her on, this Stephanie whoever she is, making false promises before he dropped her like a hot potato. The poor girl is heart-broken."

"There are two sides to every story," Kimberly said

in Jaxon's defense, "and you're only reading Stephanie's side."

"That's because you haven't shared Jaxon's side with us."

"Did I have to?" Kimberly spat back. "Forgive me if I wanted to keep some information about our relationship to myself." She rose from the table.

"That's not fair, Kim," Gabrielle replied.

"The two of you ganging up on me is not fair," Kimberly said as she began to walk away from the table.

"Oh, no, you don't." Robyn rose and grabbed her by the arm. "So you knew about this, this Stephanie person?"

"Of course I did," Kimberly said. "Do you think I would just blindly fall into bed with a man?"

"All right, all right, let's all settle down." Gabrielle tried being the voice of reason. "Guests are watching."

Suddenly Kimberly remembered her surroundings and noticed a few people were staring at them. She pursed her lips. "Fine."

Once they were all seated, Robyn wasted no time firing off a question. "How long have you known?"

"I didn't know initially," Kimberly replied tartly. "But before we became intimate, he shared his story with me and what happened between him and Stephanie."

"Clearly you felt comfortable after that to embark on a relationship with him," Gabrielle said. "But why didn't you at least tell us who he was? That's what irks us the most. I mean, maybe what happened with Stephanie isn't our business, even though we're your girls and only want what's best for you. But at the very least you could have told us his connection with the Dunhams. We've been worried sick about the gala and now we know you've had the inside scoop all along."

Kimberly turned to Gabby. "I don't have any *inside* scoop. I told Jaxon to pick the Belleza only if he thinks we're the best fit for the gala. I don't want him to choose us because he's sleeping with me." She whispered the last sentence so no one would hear them.

"Ah, now there's the Kimberly I know and love," Robyn said, breathing a sigh of relief.

"I'm sorry I didn't tell you guys about Jaxon, but our relationship caught me off guard. I wasn't expecting…"

"To fall in love," Robyn offered.

Kimberly glanced up at her and she knew in that moment that she could no longer deny how she felt any more than she could stop breathing. These were her oldest and dearest friends in the world and if she couldn't be honest with them, who could she be honest with?

Tears sprang to her eyes, but she couldn't say the words aloud. She merely nodded her head.

Robyn and Gabrielle instantly scooted their chairs over to her and wrapped their arms around her.

After several minutes, Robyn spoke. "And how does he feel about you?"

"I don't know," Kimberly answered honestly as a tear fell down her cheek.

"Then he's treating you the same way he did Stephanie, leading you on."

Kimberly shook her head, even though she'd thought the very same thing a few moments ago as she walked over to breakfast. "No, Jaxon never made me any promises, and he didn't make Stephanie any, either."

"So he's a serial dater?" Gabrielle scoffed. "You've got to be kidding me."

Robyn glared at Gabrielle before turning back to Kimberly. "Okay, he hasn't made you any promises, so no harm, no foul. You can still get out of this with your dignity intact. End it, Kimberly. End it before he breaks your heart, too."

Kimberly rose suddenly from the table. "I have to get to the office. I'll see you both later at the staff meeting." She didn't bother to hear their responses; she just rushed across the pool pavement as fast as she could in her peep-toe pumps.

As much as she wanted to go to Jaxon and talk to him, she had more pressing matters to deal with. She had to meet with the insurance adjuster at the Ruby Retreat.

Fire insurance coverage was part of the property insurance policy the Belleza had, so all the damages would be covered after their twenty-five-thousand-dollar deductible was met. The adjuster gave Kimberly the names of several licensed contractors that would accept their insurance, and thankfully, the contractor who'd done their renovations five years ago was on that list.

Kimberly never got a chance to talk with Jaxon because one meeting led to another and another. He hadn't been far from her thoughts whether she was talking to the adjuster, discussing a potential update to the Ruby Retreat's look with the contractor, meeting with the private investigator or walking the property with the landscaper on new plant choices for the front entranceway. Jaxon called her once on her mobile and sent her a few texts, which she'd been unable to respond to.

At the staff meeting later that afternoon, she made it clear to everyone that she wouldn't tolerate hearing any rumors about the curse of the Belleza.

"C'mon, Kim," Antoine, her assistant manager, said, "you have to admit that the Belleza has a haunted past."

"A curse doesn't exist," she said firmly. Then she looked around the room. "And I need you all to foster this sentiment."

"What about Trina Erickson's birthday party?" Robyn asked. "I received a formal request for a proposal from her."

Kimberly rolled her eyes upward. She wished she could give Trina the same amount of courtesy she'd shown them over the years—none—but that would be unprofessional. "Have you prepared something?"

Robyn nodded. "I did." She handed Kimberly the presentation packet.

Kimberly quickly skimmed over it. "Looks good. Send it out and let's see if she bites."

"Will do," Robyn replied.

Once the meeting concluded, she didn't stay in the conference room to talk to the girls even though she knew they wanted to talk her, not just about Trina's request, but about Jaxon, too. But until she and Jaxon hashed things out, she couldn't speak to them again.

By the time she made it back to her desk, it was well after 5:00 p.m. and she still needed to go through the nearly hundred emails waiting for her. It was going to be a long night.

Jaxon was worried. It wasn't like Kimberly not to call or at least text. She was always very responsive. Could another incident have occurred? If so, he hadn't heard anything. Was she mad at him for some reason? But he couldn't think of a single reason. Last night, they'd shared a fun night, laughing, talking and watching movies. It had been very platonic. He'd shown her that there was more to their relationship than just the physical.

Was that the reason she hadn't called? Had she really wanted him to make love to her and he'd offended her by not taking her to bed? Well, he would rectify that problem tonight.

Unfortunately he had Dunham Foundation business to attend to. He joined the conference call just as Hayley was going through roll call.

"Glad to see you could join us," his father said when Jaxon answered after his name was called.

He didn't respond; he just listened to the updates on old business from previous meetings. One of the outstanding items was the location for the Dunham Foundation annual gala.

"We have to decide," his mother stated. "We're running out of time."

"Well, perhaps if you weren't so picky," his grandmother Ruth admonished, "we wouldn't be in this position." The two women had always been at odds. His mother thought Ruth considered her high maintenance even though Ruth was the very person who'd pushed his father into marriage.

"I'm not picky. I'm selective, Mother Dunham. And there is a new hotel, The Pinnacle, opening up soon that we might want to consider."

"Do we really want to go with an unproven hotel? I've looked at all the other options," Jaxon said, "and I think the Belleza is the perfect fit."

"Is there a reason you think so, brother?" Hayley teased him.

"If you must know, yes," Jaxon responded. "Not only does the Belleza have the history and reputation to back it up rather than an upstart like The Pinnacle, it's just a two-hour drive from Los Angeles, so our guests will not have far to travel. And the hotel's grand ballroom is spectacular. I believe you visited, Hales?"

"Jack's right," she admitted. "The Belleza's grand ballroom is breathtaking and the staff took great care to show what our event might look like. You all have their presentation packet and the photos that were taken. I was impressed."

"I think we should take it to a vote," his father commented, "so we can put this matter to bed."

His mother interrupted, but his father stopped her.

"It's time, Claire," he said.

"Very well, then."

Hayley completed the call for the vote. Despite his mother's initial qualms, the decision was unanimous. The Belleza would hold the Dunham Foundation gala.

Business moved on. They continued a heated discussion on grants and eventually agreed to support the Second Harvest Food Bank since it was a local homegrown organization. They would fund the fight against autism in next year's budget.

After new business was concluded, Jaxon was about to get off the conference call, but his father stopped him. "A word, Jaxon. Everyone else can leave."

Jaxon heard the voices of the family as they said their goodbyes and left the room.

"I've put up with your insolence long enough, Jaxon," his father said. "You've made your point that as your parents we've disappointed you, but your presence, or should I say lack thereof, has been noted at several meetings with our top clients. As much as you're handling their interests, from wherever you are, they expect a face-to-face when they're in town at the end of the month. Should I tell them we can expect you?"

Jaxon hated having his arm twisted. "I'll be back." And with that he ended the call. The end of the month was in a few days. Now he had to figure out what his next move was.

Kimberly wasn't looking forward to the conversation she needed to have with Jaxon. She hated to put him on the spot, but she had to know where she stood and where their relationship was going. On the other hand, she wasn't ready to end it as Robyn had suggested. Any time she spent with Jaxon was precious and she didn't want to give it up despite how much it might hurt to know that he didn't love her as she much as she loved him.

He arrived on her doorstep at nearly 9:00 p.m. After getting home an hour earlier, she'd just had time to shower and put on a silk romper with a splash of perfume before she opened the door.

"Hey, babe." He leaned down for a kiss.

"Hi, yourself." She kept the kiss brief and pulled away, opening the door wider. "C'mon in."

She noticed the disappointed look on his face at her greeting when he walked inside, but it disappeared when he turned back to her.

"So what would you like to do tonight?" he asked, reaching for her and circling his arms around her waist.

She wiggled free of his grasp. "Actually, I thought we could talk first." She walked over to the couch and took a seat.

"Talk?" He looked perplexed and a bit bewildered by her rejection. "Okay, what would you like to talk about?"

He sat beside her, but she shifted away from him slightly. When they were close, it was too easy to fall under the spell of the strong attraction between them; he'd have her on her back before she'd get a word out. Some physical distance would help keep her mind clear and on the task at hand.

She looked at him and answered his question. "Stephanie. Us."

His brows furrowed at the name and he remained silent.

Now that the moment was here, Kimberly was nervous

as hell. "Well, we've never really talked about us, and I guess I don't want to get into the same situation that you had with Stephanie. I saw the *Beverly Hills Times* society pages today, as did my friends."

"So they know who I am?"

She nodded. "If your family finds out where you are, it won't have come from them."

"I know that. But let me guess. They were worried after reading what happened between me and Stephanie? And now you are, too?"

She nodded.

"Kimberly, my story has changed. Stephanie and I started out as childhood friends. We grew up together, but our parents wanted to play matchmaker, and to appease them, we played along and in doing so became lovers. I thought it couldn't hurt. I mean Stephanie was a good-looking girl, but I never made any commitment of any kind to her. I was up-front with Stephanie that I didn't want to marry. I'm sorry if she got the wrong impression."

Kimberly stared back at Jaxon. Was she behaving the same as Stephanie? Had she gotten the wrong impression because the attraction between them was so strong?

Jaxon eyed Kim warily. This conversation had sprung up on him out of the blue. How had they gotten here that quickly? They'd only been seeing each other for a couple of weeks. Was Kimberly like Stephanie? Was she another frantic woman in desperate need of a husband? No. Kim was nothing like Stephanie. Kim was a career-minded person like himself, strong and independent, while Stephanie was a trust-fund baby. Kimberly didn't have a manipulative bone in her body. She wanted reassurance; she wanted to hear how he felt about her, but he wasn't sure he understood his feelings, so how could he voice them?

He scooted toward her. He wouldn't let her put distance between them, especially because her fears about Stephanie were unfounded. "Listen, there was never anything substantial between me and Stephanie. Nothing other than sex. Stephanie seems to have gone on this media rampage out of spite. You can't believe a word she says."

Kim's next question was bold and direct. "Do you consider what *we* have to be 'substantial'?"

His answer was to reach across the couch, sweep Kimberly into his arms and kiss her with all the pent-up passion he'd felt since yesterday. He didn't speak; he just picked her up off the couch and carried her toward the bedroom.

"Jaxon, wait!"

But he didn't wait; he kicked open the door with his foot, and without turning on the lights, he strolled over to her bed. Not letting her go, he laid her down, framing her face and kissing her deeply. His tongue flicked out to moisten her lips and they parted, allowing him entry just as he began attacking the buttons on her romper. He sent them flying as he went after her with a hunger and urgency he hadn't known possible. He stripped her until she was naked.

He must have succeeded in changing the topic of conversation, because she murmured, "Hurry."

He removed his clothes in lightning speed. When he was just as naked as she, he put on a condom and joined her on the bed. His heart thudded loudly in his chest and a flood of sensations overtook him as he gazed down at her. Tangling his fingers in her hair, he tugged her toward him so he could glide the tip of his tongue across the fullness of her mouth. When she let out a soft moan, he used the opportunity to take advantage and feast on her hungrily. Their mouths locked together and he devoured her as if he was a starving man and she was his banquet.

A part of his brain told him that their union should be slow and gentle, but he knew it was going to be fast and hard. He teased her sweet folds aside and found her wet, and his muscles tightened with desire. He began stroking her, ardently fondling her womanhood, giving her his undivided, singular focus.

"Jaxon…" she murmured in a tortured groan.

When she could take no more and he could feel the rumble of a scream coming on, he gripped her hips and in one quick movement he entered her. An electrical charge went right through him as he surged inside her. He let out a ragged breath as he joined their bodies as one.

"Wrap your legs around me," he barked.

Kimberly did as she was told, taking him all the way inside her. He moved back and forth inside her and she lifted her hips off the bed as he pumped. She was plotting a course to send him soaring to the ultimate experience and he was happy to be on the ride.

She let out an intense scream at his final thrust and it caused his entire body to splinter. He hollered out her name and thrust one final time into her welcoming body.

The impact was so strong, so powerful, that afterward, once their breathing had returned to normal, he asked, "Was that substantial enough for you?"

Chapter 17

"That was beyond substantial," Kimberly muttered. It was cataclysmic. It was as though he'd reached inside her to her very core and touched her like no man ever had. She knew she was forever changed. There was no other man for her but Jaxon; she just wished he could see what was so obvious to her. They were made for each other.

Instead he said, "I hope you know that I truly care for you, Kimberly. This isn't just meaningless sex for me."

She appreciated him saying that, but caring for her and loving her were two entirely different things. But her pride would not let her show her disappointment. She snuggled closer into the comfort of his solid chest and that was where she slept.

When she turned over the next morning, she found Jaxon carrying a tray toward the bed.

"Good morning, sleepyhead." He settled the tray on her lap when she sat up and stacked several pillows back against the headboard.

"Is this all for me?" She looked down at the turkey bacon, egg whites, wheat toast and fresh fruit with black coffee on her lap.

"Yep." He smiled and he joined her on the bed. "I thought you might need your energy after last night." His eyes bored into hers, reminding her of the different positions in which they'd made love last night. He'd been voracious for her and she had the sore thighs to prove it. He'd definitely shown her how much he desired and wanted her.

But is that enough?

She ignored the voice inside her head. Instead, she thanked him and bit into a piece of melon. The juice ran down her face and Jaxon leaned over to lick it off her chin. "Don't you start." She wagged a finger at him. "Or you'll make me late."

"Would that be a bad thing?"

"Some of us don't make our own schedules like you do."

"Yeah, well, my days are numbered," Jaxon replied. She noticed he looked as if he'd let the cat out of the bag.

Kimberly's heart began pounding in her chest. Did that mean he was leaving the Belleza? She tried to sound calm and nonchalant even though she was far from it when she asked, "Are you leaving soon?"

He nodded reluctantly. "I have to get back to Dunham Investments. I was going to tell you, but I was trying to find the right time."

"When?" She picked at the toast.

"Soon, but let's not worry about that." He leaned over to nuzzle her neck. "What do you say to a romantic dinner later tonight at The Pearl?"

"Okay." As usual, his kisses caused heat to form below her waist and she could feel herself weakening. So it came as no surprise when Jaxon took the tray, put it on the floor and made love to her again for the second time that morning.

When Kimberly made it to work later that morning, she found she had a visitor. Her father was sitting in her guest chair.

"Daddy? What are you doing here?" she asked, walking behind her desk and taking a seat.

"I had to come," her father replied sternly, "especially when my own daughter doesn't bother to tell me there's been a fire at the Belleza."

Guilt registered across her face, but she tried to cover it. "I'm handling it."

"Handling it?" he asked, his voice booming. "When a private investigator contacts me about who my enemies might be or who might hold a grudge against my family, I think that means you far from have this matter under control."

"That's not fair." Kimberly rose from her chair and paced the room. "You placed me in charge of the Belleza because you know my business acumen. So kindly allow me to do my job."

Her father jumped up from his chair. "Don't get haughty with me, young lady. I may not run this place anymore, but your mother and I are majority shareholders and as such have a right to know if our investment is in jeopardy."

"The Belleza is not in jeopardy." Kimberly turned around to face him. She would not be intimidated by the tone in his voice. Years ago, she might have been, but not now. "I don't feel the need to share with my investors the hotel's daily comings and goings. I'm quite capable of finding out who is behind the bad reviews and the *small* fire at the Ruby Retreat."

Her father seemed surprised that she was not backing down or kowtowing to him. "And you're sure it's not Sean?"

Kimberly rolled her eyes. "C'mon, Daddy. Even you must see how ludicrous that sounds. He would never set fire to the Belleza. It's his inheritance as much as it is mine. Not to mention, you and Mama just made up, so you shouldn't be going there again."

Her father shrugged. "Then you have a big problem on your hands."

"Nothing I can't deal with," she responded. "That's why I hired an investigator. We'll get to the bottom of this."

"You're that confident?"

She nodded. "I am, but I need you not to lose faith in me and my abilities."

"I do have faith in you."

Her eyebrow shot up. "Do you really? Or are you just telling me what you think I want to hear?"

"No, I'm not," he stated more firmly. "And I promise not to stick my nose where it doesn't belong, if you promise to keep us abreast so I'm not blindsided when some detective shows up at my door."

"Fair enough." She offered her hand. "Deal?"

Instead of accepting her handshake, her father pulled her into a firm hug. "Deal. I love you, Kim."

"Love you, too, Daddy."

Jaxon walked into The Pearl later that afternoon to meet with Gabrielle.

He could see she was surprised because she came out in her cap and executive-chef coat.

"Jaxon Dunham."

He smiled even though he knew she wasn't pleased by his hiding his real identity. "Yes. How are you, Gabrielle?"

"That depends on why you're here," she replied with a skeptical look. "What can I do for you?"

"I would like to have the private room tonight," he said, pointing toward the glass doors.

"We only use that for our monthly tasting menu or for large parties," Gabrielle replied.

"I'm sure. But tonight is special. I want to show Kimberly just how important she is to me."

"That's good, because I don't want her to get hurt."

"And you think I would hurt her?"

"Robyn and I saw the newspaper article."

"But that's not the only reason you have your doubts?" He suspected there was more to her concern. His cell phone rang in his pocket and Jaxon pulled it out, saw that it was his mother and put it back into his pocket. He didn't have time to deal with her. This was more important.

Gabrielle shrugged. "C'mon, Jaxon, we travel in the same circles and although we've never met, I've heard a lot about you. You're the bachelor that every socialite wants to snag. It's easy to see how your ex-girlfriend could get the wrong idea."

"I know I have a reputation, but I've always been upfront with the women I'm with, including Kimberly. I'm not using her, if that's what you're implying, Gabrielle. I care for her."

At that comment, Gabrielle's demeanor began to warm. "That's good to hear and of course because your request is for Kim, I'll agree, but you'll have to pay top dollar to have exclusive use of the room. Though I'm sure that's no problem for a Dunham."

Jaxon gritted his teeth to keep from pointing out that he'd made his own money and didn't depend on the Dunham name or bank account. He didn't want to antagonize her, not when he needed a favor. "That brings me to my second request."

"Which is?"

"I would like a special menu in our honor."

Gabrielle glanced down at her watch; it was 3:00 p.m. "You sure don't want much, do you?"

"I'm sure a top-notch executive chef such as yourself is used to the unexpected. You'll take care of it?" he asked, but it was more like a statement. He knew that at the Belleza, the staff prided themselves on catering to their exclusive guests.

Gabrielle narrowed her eyes at him, but she placed a smile on her face and said, "Of course."

"Great. We'll be here at seven," Jaxon said. He turned to leave, but spun around. "I really appreciate this, Gabrielle, and I know Kimberly will, too."

She inclined her head in acknowledgment.

Jaxon smiled as he left The Pearl. The stage was set for a private romantic dinner. Even though he had to leave soon, he hoped tonight would show her how he felt and would ease her mind. He wasn't ready to put a name to his feelings for her yet, but he wasn't ready to give her up, either. He just hoped Kimberly would understand.

Kimberly paid special care when she dressed for her date with Jaxon that evening. She'd found a simple spaghetti-strap jersey dress in the back of her closet. It was flaming red, but it would give her the confidence boost she needed. She wasn't sure what the evening was all about, but she would look fabulous nonetheless. She added gold hoops to her ears, a three-teardrop necklace to her neck and strappy red sandals on her feet as her final accessory before spritzing her favorite perfume.

Jaxon arrived at six forty-five wearing a black suit and a crisp white shirt with a few buttons open at the top. He looked sexier than any man had a right to be and she swallowed.

"Hey, beautiful." He twirled her around as he entered her condo so he could get a better look at her.

She could see the appreciative look in his eye and it made her feel sexy.

He offered her his arm. "Ready to go?"

"Yes."

Minutes later, they were in his Jaguar riding over to The Pearl. She would have been just fine in her golf cart, but Jaxon had insisted on the car as they were having a "proper date."

When they arrived at The Pearl, the hostess Charlene was there to greet them. "Ms. P-P-Parker," she stammered. "I—I had no idea you were coming." She was clearly unnerved at seeing her boss after-hours.

"We have a reservation under Jack Scott," Jaxon said, attempting to get her back on track.

Charlene glanced down at her book. "Oh, okay. I see it." She pointed down to her book. "I just assumed... Well, never mind." She grabbed two menus and started walking toward the main dining room. "I'll show you to a table."

"No, no." Jaxon stopped her. "We have the private room." He pointed to the glass door behind Charlene.

"What?" Kimberly and Charlene both looked at him, perplexed.

"That's for groups," Charlene said.

"And I arranged it with Gabrielle earlier," Jaxon said. "Do you need to check your book again?"

Charlene rushed back toward the hostess stand. "Oh, yeah. I mean, oh, yes, you're right, Mr. Scott, My apologies." She placed the menus back in the bin. "I see a note from the executive chef. Please follow me."

She walked them to the private room. Once there, Kimberly could see that the large table had been replaced with a single circular table set for two, along with what looked like a special menu.

Charlene attempted to pull out Kimberly's chair, but stumbled.

"I'll take it from here," Jaxon replied, taking over and helping Kimberly to her seat. "Thank you."

"Enjoy your evening." Charlene waved on her way out, but she wasn't paying attention and slammed right into the glass door. "Oops, my bad." She laughed and managed to open the door with no further issues.

"Is she always like that?" Jaxon asked as he came around to sit opposite her.

Kimberly shrugged. She didn't want to think about Charlene, only Jaxon and how thoughtful he'd been in arranging this private dinner. "I can't believe you arranged all this."

Jaxon smiled widely, showing off his white teeth. "I have my moments."

"I can see that," Kimberly said, placing her napkin in her lap.

"Champagne?" he asked, glancing at the bottle chilling in a bucket beside the table.

"I'd love some."

Jaxon easily popped the cork, then filled two flutes. "For you." He handed her the glass and touched his to hers.

"You're a special lady, Kimberly Parker," he said. "And I wanted you to know it."

Kimberly smiled. Now if he could only say the three words she so desperately wanted to hear, everything would be right in the world.

In addition to their always stimulating conversation, they enjoyed a delectable three-course meal that Gabrielle had prepared exclusively for them. They started with a pear and kale salad with radishes, red endive, caramelized honey and pistachio-crusted goat cheese beignets. It was followed by red snapper with polenta and broccolini, and a decadent dessert of caramel-apple pie with pecan streusel and persimmon sherbet. The meal was to die for.

Kimberly was thankful to Jaxon and Gabby for such a great evening. They were enjoying their dessert when the glass doors to the private room swung open and a beautiful, tall woman burst in.

She had big eighties-style highlighted brown hair that reached her shoulders and was clad in a belted jumpsuit and spiky stilettos.

"So this is where you've been hiding out!" she yelled, "You lying dog!"

The stunned look on Jaxon's face told Kimberly exactly who the woman was before he even said her name. "Stephanie, what the hell are you doing here? And how did you find me?"

Charlene came rushing in behind Stephanie looking sheepish. "I'm so sorry, Ms. Parker. She barged in and wouldn't take no for answer."

Kimberly held her hand up to stop the young woman from chattering any more. "It's okay, Charlene. I've got this."

Charlene nodded and hung her head apologetically as she closed the door behind her.

"I didn't hunt you down if that's what you're insinuating," Stephanie replied. "Your parents told me where you are."

"Excuse me?" Jaxon quickly rose to his feet.

"Apparently you're not as slick as you think you are at hiding your tracks."

"You should leave, Stephanie," Jaxon said. "You're not welcome here and this is entirely inappropriate."

"Ha!" She laughed and threw her head back. "Clearly, because you have another piece on the side to satisfy your sexual needs. My God, Jaxon. Have you no shame?"

"Who should be ashamed is you," he responded. "You're the one who's been smearing my name, my family's name all over the local tabloids. And to what end, Stephanie? You know as well as I do that marriage was never on the table."

"That's bull, Jaxon, and you know it," Stephanie said. "You led me on. You had me and my family believing we had a future."

"I never made you any promises."

"Are you kidding me?" She chuckled bitterly. "You didn't seem to mind when you were in my bed. In fact, you couldn't seem to get enough of this." She slid her hands down the sides of her curvaceous body. There was no disguising the woman had a banging body and Kimberly could see she'd dressed tonight with the sole purpose of showing Jaxon exactly what he was missing.

"That's enough." Jaxon glanced in Kimberly's direction and he could no doubt read the emotion on her face at seeing Stephanie's pain.

It was evident to Kimberly that Stephanie had feelings for Jaxon even though he may not have shared them. It was like looking in a mirror. Tears began to well in Kimberly's eyes. Was history repeating itself? Was she as deluded as Stephanie that the incredible lovemaking they shared could somehow lead to something more real, something more substantial?

"I'll say when it's enough," Stephanie replied. "She—" Stephanie pointed to Kimberly "—needs to know who you truly are. She needs to know that she's fooling herself if she thinks you're ever going to commit to her, because you won't."

Stephanie turned to Kimberly this time. "He's a liar and a user. And when he's finished with you, he'll toss you aside and leave you brokenhearted."

"I've had enough of you. You've no right to come here and dump all your emotional baggage and insecurities on me and Kimberly. You're just angry and hurt that you're not *the one*." Jaxon started toward Stephanie, but she held her hands up in the air.

"Don't you touch me, don't you dare touch me," she snapped. "I've said what I came here to say. I've looked you in the face and told you exactly what I think of you. The great Jaxon Dunham is nothing but a lying dog and I hope you rot in hell."

She turned on her heel and stormed out of the room, rattling the glass door on her way out with the force of her exit.

"Kimberly," Jaxon began, but she put up her hands in defensive mode.

"Don't!" She glanced outside the glass door and could see they had an audience. All the other diners had seen the encounter.

"I'm so sorry that Stephanie came here and ruined what would otherwise have been an amazing night."

Kimberly shook her head. She was confused and needed some air. "I have to go." She didn't wait to hear any more; she just rushed from the room. She heard Gabby calling her name as she fled from The Pearl, but she just wanted to be alone.

Chapter 18

Kimberly didn't make it very far from the dining area. She'd run as far as the main lawn before Jaxon caught up to her.

"Kimberly, wait!"

She stopped in the middle of the lawn, but didn't look at him. Tears were streaming down her cheeks and she didn't want him to see her like this. To know how invested she was, to know how much Stephanie's words had hurt. "Go away!"

"No!" Jaxon spun her around. When he saw her tears, he wiped them away with the pads of his thumbs. "Please don't cry." He tried to pull her into an embrace, but Kimberly pushed away from him.

"Don't do that. It won't make it better."

"Kim?"

"I thought I understood," she began. "But after meeting Stephanie, I see there's another side to the story."

"So you believe her? And all the hateful things she was spewing out?"

Kimberly shook her head. "Not all of it, but she was speaking from a place of hurt."

"You know I never intended any of that to happen. She and I agreed to a casual relationship to appease our parents. Nothing more."

"The thing is, Jaxon, that's easier said than done. And whether you intended it or not, you hurt her."

"But I never said that I loved her. How could she jump to the conclusion that I wanted more, that I wanted marriage?"

Kimberly was troubled. "You don't get it, do you?" she screamed. "You didn't have to! She got caught up in the moment, in being with you, and if it was anything like you and I..." Her voice trailed off.

His nostrils flared. "You and Stephanie are nothing alike. What *we*—" he pointed back and forth between them "—share is nothing alike."

"What am I to you, Jaxon?" Kimberly blurted out.

At his perplexed expression, she tried again. "How do you feel about me, Jaxon? Am I just another momentary pleasure, a casual relationship that you can toss aside when it's time to go back to the family fold?"

Jaxon looked like a deer caught in the headlights. "You know how I feel about you, Kimberly. I showed you last night."

"Do I? For that matter, do *you*?"

Jaxon was at a momentary loss for words. He hadn't expected Kimberly to come at him so hard and put him on the spot about his feelings. He'd been having trouble sorting them out himself. Hadn't he told Kimberly that he *cared* for her and that she was important to him? Hadn't he created this entire evening to show her how much? Why was that not enough?

He wished Stephanie had never shown up. If she hadn't, he and Kimberly wouldn't be on this conversation path, or at least not until he was good and ready.

And now Kimberly was looking at him with those puppy-dog eyes and begging him to say something, to say anything, but he was frozen, frozen in fear. He'd never told a woman he loved her before. And Jaxon wasn't sure he ever could.

Disappointment shone in Kimberly's eyes as she stared at Jaxon. She was hoping, praying that he would tell her he loved her, tell her that what they shared mattered to him, but he couldn't, wouldn't, and now she had to do the one thing she feared most. She had to let him go.

She nodded. "It's okay, it's okay," she began, nodding her head as if she'd come to some kind of decision. "You don't have to say anything."

"Kim—"

"I owe you an apology."

A bewildered look spread across his face. "Apology?"

"Yes, because you were up-front from the beginning about how you felt about commitment. You told me that you weren't interested in a relationship. You made that perfectly clear tonight with Stephanie." Kimberly pointed back to the Plaza. "But I didn't listen. And I'm to blame. I said I was okay with living in the moment."

"But you can't?"

She nodded. "No, I can't. I can't do it anymore, Jaxon. I can't act like I haven't come to care for you. I can't act like making love with you and lying beside you each and every night doesn't mean anything to me. I can't act like I don't love you, Jaxon, because I would be lying to you and to myself most of all."

Jaxon's eyes became as large as saucers at her admission of love. Clearly, she'd stunned him. "I—I'm so sorry, Kimberly. I had no idea. I never—"

But she cut him off. "Please, don't apologize. It just makes it worse. It makes me feel like a fool when you made your intentions perfectly clear."

"Can you just give me some time to figure this out? I mean, does it have to be all-or-nothing, right this second?"

"Actually, it does, because either you love me or you don't."

When he remained silent, Kimberly could see it was a stalling tactic. She didn't wait for his answer because she already knew what it was. He didn't love her. She took off running and this time Jaxon didn't come after her.

"She has to be in there."

From inside her condo, Kimberly heard Robyn's voice at her door. She hadn't been out or at work in two days, nor had she answered her phone. Now her friends were out there knocking on her door, and from the sound of it, they were persistent.

"Kim, honey, you need to open the door, because we are not going to go away."

That was Gabrielle.

"You know we can have this door opened," Robyn threatened. "And we're not above pulling rank over the staff, so please just open up."

Kimberly surrendered. She swung the door open, despite the fact that she was wearing her pajamas and her hair was a tangled mess. As soon as she saw her friends, her face crumpled into tears and she bent over as if in physical pain.

Robyn and Gabrielle rushed forward and caught her before she fell to the ground. "We've got you." Robyn grabbed hold of one of her arms while Gabrielle took the other and they helped her to the sofa.

Kimberly curled into a ball on the sofa and bawled.

"Kim, what happened?" Robyn asked.

"We know you and Jaxon quarreled with another

woman at The Pearl the other night," Gabrielle answered.
"Who was she? Did something happen after? Did she accost you guys outside the restaurant?"

Kimberly was silent as she cried, so Robyn walked over to the settee by the door, grabbed the tissue box and came back over. She handed it to Kimberly and she took several tissues and blew her nose.

Her friends were quiet as they waited for her response. "She didn't accost us," Kimberly finally said. "She didn't have to. Her appearance at dinner was like a bomb. It completely decimated me."

"Dear God!" Robyn's hand flew to her mouth at the metaphor.

"Who was she?" Gabrielle pressed. "Wait, let me guess…was she Jaxon's ex?"

Kimberly nodded.

Gabrielle glanced at Robyn and they both nodded in understanding.

"Seeing her in person was different than just listening to a story of a woman scorned," Kimberly replied. "It made her *real* and the feelings she had for Jaxon were just that real. But he didn't see it, refused to."

"So you guys had a fight about her?" Gabrielle said. "If that's the worst that happened, you can kiss and make up, right? I hear makeup sex is the best." As soon as she said it, Gabrielle realized she'd put her foot in her mouth, because fresh tears began to roll down Kimberly's cheeks again. "I'm so sorry, sweetie… I—"

"It's not your fault that I entered into casual sex with Jaxon. He made it abundantly clear at the outset that he was a no-strings-attached kind of guy, but I got so caught up in the amazing, earth-shattering sex that I let my guard down. I let him inside my heart." She shook her head.

"And what?" Robyn asked.

"And I fell in love with him," Kimberly cried. "But he didn't fall in love with me. I asked him last night and he just stood there, like a statue, while I poured my heart out to him."

"I'm so sorry." Robyn reached for Kimberly and pulled her into an embrace. She rubbed Kimberly's back when sobs began to rack her body.

"He doesn't want me," Kimberly said, clutching Robyn's shirt.

"It'll be okay." Gabrielle reached for Kimberly's hand. "We'll get you through this. You are not alone. I promise you, Kim. It may not feel that way now, but you're not alone."

Kimberly looked up at Robyn and Gabrielle through the haze of her tears. "Thank you."

"I bet we can cheer you up," Robyn said.

"I doubt that's possible." Kimberly sniffed.

"What if I told you that Trina rejected our proposal for her birthday celebration? Said it wasn't high-class enough for her. Can you believe that?"

Now, that brought a smile to Kimberly's face. "Well, good riddance. The Pinnacle can have her and her high-class party because we—" she pointed to her friends "—don't need her business."

"Never have," Gabrielle offered.

"And never will," Robyn finished.

Jaxon glanced through the back window at the Belleza as the limousine drove away. He'd checked out this morning and was on his way back to Beverly Hills. After last night, he didn't feel as though he had any choice. It had hurt him to see Kimberly so distraught knowing he was the cause of her pain. But he'd been unable to stop himself. She'd asked him point-blank how he felt about her, if he'd fallen in love with her, but he'd been unable to say the words back to her. And he didn't understand why.

Maybe if he went home and dealt with the unfinished business he had back there he could figure out the reason. Maybe it would help explain why he'd just turned his back on an incredible woman like Kimberly Parker. She was the entire package. Beautiful. Intelligent. Sexy. Confident. Caring. He'd been a fool to let her run away last night, but he'd been so closed off for years that he wasn't sure he knew how to be the man she needed him to be. Until he did, she was better off without him. No matter how much he might miss her, crave her, need her beside him, underneath him. He had to work out his issues. Once he did, then he could come back to her and look her in the face and tell her everything she deserved to hear.

Kimberly made her way into the office. Her assistant had been shocked when she'd called in sick yesterday and asked Antoine to take over the staff meeting, but she needed time to get her head on straight. Yesterday had been quite cathartic for her. She'd cried until she didn't think there were any more tears left. Robyn and Gabrielle had stayed by her side for a while and then they'd had to get back to work, but each alternated checking on her throughout the day. She didn't know what she would do without them. Right now, they were her lifeline.

She went through the motions of the staff meeting that afternoon until they reviewed the departures and arrivals of their important guests.

Emily Halverson, head of Reservations, gave her report. "Mr. Scott checked out yesterday, so his villa is now ready for the Simpson family coming in later today."

Kimberly looked up from the notes she'd been writing. "Excuse me?"

"You remember Mr. Scott? He'd been staying here for nearly two months," Emily responded. "He checked out yesterday."

Kimberly nodded in acknowledgment and tears began to bite at her eyes. She rose and walked over to the conference room window and kept her back to her staff. "Umm...we're done for today."

"But we haven't finished yet," Antoine interrupted her.

"We'll take care of any pressing issues," Robyn and Gabrielle said simultaneously and several staff members looked at them in alarm.

"Meeting is adjourned," Robyn said and glanced at Kimberly's hunched back.

Once everyone had left the room, Gabrielle closed the door and they both rushed over to her side.

"He's gone?" Kimberly's hand flew to her mouth as she held back a sob. "Wow! I didn't see that coming."

She'd foolishly thought that after he'd had some time to think about it, he would come to her and admit he loved her, but he hadn't. After she'd poured her heart out to him, he couldn't hightail it fast enough out of the Belleza. Her confession of love must have been so uncomfortable for him to hear that he'd had to flee like a thief from the scene of the crime.

"I'm sorry, Kimberly," Robyn replied. "Jaxon is showing his true colors right now. I know you need to cry and get it out, but he's not worthy of your tears if he failed to realize what a truly spectacular woman you are."

"I know that up here," Kimberly said, pointing to her head, "but it still hurts here." She pointed to her chest. "Maybe if I hadn't pressured him..."

"He wouldn't have left?" Gabrielle finished. "Don't

delude yourself, my friend. Jaxon is afraid of commitment. Better you realize it now before you get any deeper into the relationship like Stephanie. You wouldn't want to end up like her, all cold and bitter and vindictive."

Kimberly stared at Gabrielle. She had a point. But she could never see herself behaving as Stephanie had. And she most certainly wouldn't have called him out about it in public. How embarrassing! She would lick her wounds here at the Belleza without the public's prying eyes.

"I appreciate the pep talk." Kimberly sniffed. "And I'll get through this." She didn't have much choice. Jaxon had left, making it clear to her that he wasn't interested in pursuing a future with her.

Chapter 19

"Well, if it isn't the black sheep of the family," Hayley said from the doorway of Jaxon's bedroom at the Dunham family estate. He'd been living at the estate temporarily while renovations were completed on the condominium he'd purchased a few months ago and before World War III broke out with Stephanie.

He'd just returned about a half hour ago and had gone up to his suite to unpack. Housed on the second floor of the Dunham's twenty-bedroom mansion, his suite included a bedroom, large dressing room and sitting area. "Good to see you, too, Hales," Jaxon said as he unzipped his suitcases.

"Are you sure about that?" Hayley replied with her arms folded across her chest. "I think I was the one who let your secret location slip to Mother."

Jaxon spun on his heel. "So it was you?" He turned back around and returned to unpacking his suitcase. "I was wondering how they knew and could tell Stephanie."

Hayley frowned. "Stephanie? She was there? At the Belleza?"

"Yep." Jaxon walked over to his large walk-in closet and began hanging several items of clothing. "Burst into a romantic dinner I was having and unleashed her rage on me."

"Wow! I'm so sorry about that, Jack. I had no idea." Hayley came forward and sat on the edge of his bed.

"It's not your fault," he replied. "She'd been stewing for months and wanted her pound of flesh. She got it and then some."

"How so?"

"Remember I said I was having a romantic dinner," he said, making air quotes over the last two words.

Hayley raised one eyebrow. "Have you been seeing a new woman since you've been at the Belleza? I thought you'd sworn off women after Stephanie."

"I did. Until Kimberly."

"Kimberly? Kimberly Parker? General manager of the Belleza?"

Jaxon nodded as he added a button-down shirt to a hanger. "And she didn't take too kindly to Stephanie interrupting our date. Matter of fact, the whole evening blew up in my face."

"Jeez, that doesn't sound good."

"It wasn't."

"Well, you have to do something about it."

Jaxon turned to stare at his sister. "I will, because if I don't I'm going to lose her."

Later that afternoon, when Jaxon was on his way out to run some errands, he saw the door to his father's study was open. As much as he dreaded this conversation, he couldn't avoid it indefinitely, so better he face it head-on now.

He knocked on the door and a resounding baritone voice said, "Come in."

Jaxon opened the door and walked into the masculine-looking study done in browns and beige with solid oak furniture. Shock registered on his father's face at seeing

Jaxon, but he quickly recovered and a frown replaced his initial reaction.

His father looked the same, with dark brown eyes just like Jaxon's, salt-and-pepper hair in a well-groomed fade and mustache, and his favorite weekend ensemble of cashmere sweater over dark trousers that only emphasized his broad shoulders.

"Look who decided to return," his father commented as he wrote on his notepad.

Jaxon wasn't surprised by his cold reaction. It was signature Charles Dunham. He believed family matters should be handled with an iron fist.

"Father." Jaxon didn't take the seat in front of the desk so he could be scolded like a child who'd done wrong. Instead, he walked to the window that overlooked the pond.

Silence ensued between both men for several long minutes. It was his father who spoke first. "So we can expect you back at Dunham Investments tomorrow?"

"I'll be there and I'll be helping Hales with the Dunham Foundation gala."

"Good. Was there something else?"

Jaxon spun around at the dismissive tone in the man's voice. "Actually, there is."

His harsh tone caused his father to swivel his chair around to face him. "You have something to say?"

"Don't interfere in my life again," Jaxon stated. His eyes were dark and stormy. His father returned the glare. "I've had enough of you and Mother inserting yourselves into my life."

"Perhaps if you didn't make a mess of your life, we wouldn't have to *insert* ourselves," his father responded tartly.

"I have not made a mess of my life," Jaxon replied. "But you have caused me stress and this family undue negative publicity by announcing an engagement that never existed."

"Ah, here it comes." His father rose to his feet. "We're the reason for your misfortune and the bad press. Did you ever think to look in the mirror?"

Jaxon nodded. "Oh, I've had plenty of time to look in the mirror. I don't deny that I should never have gotten involved in a casual relationship with Stephanie. Clearly she's an unstable woman and I just fueled the flames. But you and Mother made it worse."

"By wanting what's best for you? What's best for this family?" His father's voice rose several decibels. "God, you and your sister are so ungrateful. You've had everything handed to you on a silver platter and now you're whining about it?"

"What's best for me is to find *my own* way," Jaxon yelled back at him. "I'm your son. When did you stop being on my side?"

His father stared at him in shock. Before he could say anything, the door to the study burst open.

"I heard voices—" His mother stopped midsentence when she saw the other occupant of the room.

"Jaxon!" She cried and rushed toward him. She wrapped her arms around him in a hug. "Oh, thank God, you're home. I thought we'd lost you for good."

"It's okay, Mother." Jaxon patted her back. She was so petite at five foot one that sometimes he felt as if he might break her. It didn't help that it looked as if she'd lost some weight since he'd been gone. Was it stress because of him? "I'm here now."

She pulled away from him and smoothed her coiffed silver chignon as she digested his words. "For how long?"

"Honestly, I don't know," Jaxon said. And he didn't. Coming back home was like opening up a wound that hadn't quite healed yet. He'd hoped his stay at the Belleza would have helped, but it was like a scab had replaced the open wound and it was still raw.

"What's going on, Charles?" His mother looked at his father. "Why is Jaxon talking of leaving again?"

Charles Dunham shook his head. "Because he doesn't think that I'm in his corner."

His mother turned to Jaxon and touched his cheek. "You know that's not true. We love you."

"Like you love each other?" Jaxon asked and his mother's face blanched.

"What's that supposed to mean?" she inquired, taking a step back.

"You both have been in such a rush to marry me off. Why? So I can be like you two in an unhappy marriage? No thanks."

Her mother glanced at his father, who lowered his head. "Your father and I are not unhappy."

"No?" Jaxon snorted. "But you're not madly in love, either. Never have been. I don't want that kind of marriage. If I can't have the real thing, I don't want any part of it."

"We may not have a perfect marriage," his father responded, "but your mother and I have a mutual respect for each other."

"Sounds romantic," Jaxon snarled.

"Is that why you've shied away from marriage?" his mother asked. "Because of us?"

"Partly. I never felt I had a good example of one," Jaxon said.

"Marriage is what you make of it, son," his father replied. "But you have to be willing to take that risk. It's why we pushed you so hard. It can have its advantages."

"But can't you see, the more you push, the more I retreat? Trying to force an engagement on me only made me want to run and hide."

"Which is why you've been hiding out at the Belleza?" his mother asked.

"How long have you known?"

His father replied instead, "I've known for some time. I had an investigator looking for you." He continued at Jaxon's stunned expression. "Listen, I had to be sure no one had kidnapped you or something. You are the heir to a large fortune, but once I realized you were in no immediate danger, I decided to give you some space and hope you would come to your senses. And your mother, well, she just recently found out because Hayley let it slip that she'd seen you when she'd toured the Belleza for the Dunham Foundation gala."

Jaxon nodded. He'd thought he'd been careful that day, but his sister had still found him out.

"Listen, Jaxon." His mother grasped his hand. "We had no idea how unstable Stephanie was. I thought by telling her where you were that you guys could talk and clear the air. I had no idea she would behave so terribly by storming the hotel and demanding answers from you. It's made your father and I evaluate whether we want someone like her in our family."

"Your mother tried to call your cell and warn you that Stephanie was coming and that she was on the warpath, but you didn't pick up," his father said.

Jaxon remembered the call he'd gotten on his cell phone earlier that day when he'd been meeting with Gabrielle and how he'd let it go to voice mail. "Okay, so you tried to warn me and I'm sorry I didn't pick up, but that doesn't change the fact that you two stopped being in my corner. You have to stop interfering and let me live my own life."

"We know that," his mother said, "and we promise we will. If you promise not to shut us out of your life again if we make a mistake. We're not perfect, Jaxon. And despite what you may think, we love each other and we love you."

"Your mother is right," his father replied. "We love you and we promise to have your back going forward, outsiders be damned." With one hand, his father reached out and circled it around Jaxon's head, pulling him toward him. "I love you, son."

After several long moments, Jaxon patted his father's back. "I love you, too."

Jaxon was surprised. He'd never thought the conversation with his parents would be this positive, but they'd surprised him with their honesty and candor. It made him see that relationships were not perfect. They were complicated, messy and ever-evolving. It made him realize that if he didn't stop running he might miss out on the best thing that had ever happened to him. Kimberly Parker.

He drove over to Nate's place to talk over his next steps and how he could win Kimberly back after screwing up royally. He'd walked out on her after she'd told him she loved him. He'd been so stunned to hear her admission out loud that he hadn't known what to do. If he was honest with himself, he'd suspected how she felt about him. How could he not? She'd worn her heart on her sleeve. Even when they were making love, she'd been honest with her responsiveness to him. And instead of cherishing what she'd offered, he'd thrown it back in her face as if their time together had meant nothing at all. No wonder she hadn't answered any of his calls or texts.

"Hey, when did you get back?" Nate asked after Jaxon walked into his home later that afternoon. The house was theirs, since his kids were at a birthday party.

"Yesterday," Jaxon said. "Had to deal with some family business."

Nate quirked a brow. "And how did that go?"

"Got a beer?" Jaxon asked.

"Hey, the last time I drank with you, I ended up on the couch for two nights," Nate replied. "It was awfully lonely on that couch."

"Sorry about that, man," Jaxon said, following behind him. "But a lot has been going on."

"All right. C'mon, I'll take pity on you." Nate led him to the kitchen at the back of his ranch-style three-bedroom home. It had a spacious floor plan that overlooked an enormous family room, which right now had several toys scattered over the floor. Jaxon stepped over one of them as he slid onto a stool at the counter while Nate fetched two beers out of the fridge.

Once he cracked it open, he slid it toward Jaxon and he happily accepted, taking a long drag. "So," Nate said, opening a beer for himself. "What's got you all fired up?"

"Kimberly, Stephanie, my parents."

"That's a mouthful. What happened?"

"Stephanie showed up at the Belleza, where I was staying."

"The Belleza? You were that close and kept that to yourself? I have to hand it to you. That was pretty stealth."

"I know, I know," Jaxon replied, "but I needed some space to clear my head."

"But instead of finding space, you found your way into Kimberly's Parker's bed."

Jaxon smiled sheepishly. "But here's the thing, Nate. She found her way into my heart."

"What?" Nate's brow rose in surprise.

"I think I'm in love, man."

"You think or you know?"

Jaxon was silent for a long moment as he pondered the question. His mind went back to the very first time he'd seen Kimberly when she was poolside with her friends. He recalled the first time they made love and how incredible it had been. Or that highly charged encounter in the cave. If he was honest with himself, he'd known then that he loved her. He had never felt that connected with another person, but he hadn't been ready to admit his feelings to himself until now. "I know."

"What are you going to do about it?"

"I don't know." Jaxon took a swig of his beer. "I messed things up with Kimberly, Nate."

"What happened?"

He filled in his friend on Stephanie's histrionics. "Afterward, Kimberly told me that she loved me and asked me point-blank how I felt about her, but I couldn't say it back to her. That's when she told me to take a hike, that she wasn't interested in being Stephanie part *deux*."

"Ouch!"

"What do I do? You've been married for seven years. You guys have had fights. How do you recover from it?"

"This is way more than a fight, Jaxon. She broke up with you because you weren't willing to tell her those three little words that every woman wants to hear from the man she's sleeping with."

Jaxon lowered his head in despair. "How do I make it up to her?"

"You need a big gesture," Nate said, taking a swig of beer. "One that shows Kimberly exactly how you feel about her and that you're in it for the long haul."

"But what?"

"You're a smart guy. You'll figure something out."

* * *

Kimberly stared at her cell phone. Jaxon had called and left a voice mail. Actually, he'd left several over the past few days since he'd gone, but she couldn't bear to listen to any of them and had deleted each and every one of them. She was better off if they just made a clean break. No amount of talking was going to change the fact that he just wasn't that into her or at least not how she was into him. She didn't just like him. She loved him, but Jaxon didn't want or seem capable of accepting that love and she wasn't about to beat her head against a brick wall. If he didn't want her, she had to move on.

It wouldn't be easy to do, but she had to try. Work helped. Yesterday, she received a call from Cole, the R & B artist who'd attended her tasting menu last month. She hadn't much cared for him, especially the way he'd put down her staff, but he wasn't the first entitled celebrity they'd dealt with at the Belleza and he certainly wouldn't be last. The request, however, caught her off guard.

"You want us to do what?" She stared back at the receiver.

"You heard correctly," Cole said. "I need you to plan a last-minute wedding for me. My manager or publicist can't find out anything about it or they'll try to nix the nuptials. The bride is a celebrity like me, so this has to be extremely hush-hush."

"But in a day?" Kimberly asked. Sure, they'd done last-minute events before and pulling off the impossible was a knack they'd developed…but in twenty-four hours? Even Kimberly wasn't sure they could pull it off.

"You have to," Cole said. "It has to be tomorrow night."

"What about the bride? Doesn't she have a say in this? I mean, we need her input to ensure this day is all that you *both* imagined it would be."

"My bride just wants to marry me. She'll be happy with whatever you decide given your restraints."

"But why the rush?" Kimberly inquired. "If we can have at least a week, I promise you we can do more. You'll have the—"

Cole interrupted her. "We want tomorrow. Can you do it or not?"

Well, he was direct, Kimberly thought. "Let me speak with my event planner. I'll get back to you within the hour."

"Excellent. I know you won't let me down," he said before hanging up.

Kimberly immediately dialed Robyn and then Gabrielle and cryptically said, "Drop whatever you're doing. My office *now*."

In minutes, her two best friends stormed into her office with matching scowls.

"Listen, missy," Gabrielle said, as she pointed her finger at her, "I know you're going through a lot and all, but I don't appreciate being summoned when I'm in the middle of preparing one of my signature soufflés."

Robyn nodded her agreement. "What gives?"

"I just got a call from Cole," Kimberly said, glancing at the phone. She was still in disbelief at his request. "You remember him, right?"

"That obnoxious singer from last month's tasting-menu dinner?" Gabrielle asked. "How can I forget? He treated the staff like servants."

"He contacted me today and wants me to arrange his wedding."

"Is that all?" Gabrielle huffed and began walking toward the door. "He can take a number like everyone else."

"The wedding is tomorrow."

Gabrielle spun on her heels. "Excuse me?"

Robyn sank into the seat across from Kimberly and unbuttoned the top two buttons on her orange silk shirt.

"He is willing to pay us an enormous sum if we can pull off this wedding in time," Kimberly replied.

"But that's insane," Gabrielle said. "It's just not possible."

Kimberly ignored her. "It's a small wedding with approximately ten guests. How hard could it be to put a menu together and have a small cake?"

"Do you have any idea what you're asking? I'd have to be up all night," Gabrielle responded.

"I told him I would never agree to such a thing but that's when he offered each of us an outrageous sum plus 20 percent bonuses," Kimberly replied.

"How much?" Robyn wanted to know. "Because what he's asking for, in the time frame he's asking for, doesn't come cheap."

Kimberly wrote the figure on a slip of paper and passed it across the desk to Robyn. Robyn rolled her eyes before reaching for it, but when she saw the amount, she looked up in utter shock. "He's willing to pay us that much?"

Kimberly nodded. "You see, we *have* to do it."

"Wait just a minute," Gabrielle said, walking toward the desk. "My job is the hardest here. I want to know how much that jerk is willing to pay." When Robyn handed her the piece of paper, Gabrielle stopped in her tracks and looked at both of them. "We can't turn this down."

"That's exactly what I just said," Kimberly replied.

"But you didn't lead with the money," Gabrielle responded. "Next time lead with the cold hard cash."

Kimberly smiled at her friends. Although they were both paid well by the Belleza, she knew what a saver Robyn was because she never wanted to be broke ever again and end up in the projects where she came from. And Gabrielle wanted to show her parents that living well was the best revenge. "So can we do this?"

"Yes!" they both said in unison.

Kimberly was glad they were on board because it was going to take a miracle to create a wedding in one day, especially when she was heartbroken knowing hers may never come.

Chapter 20

The night of Cole's wedding arrived. All the arrangements had been made and the stage was set for romance. The past twenty-four hours had been a flurry of activity for all of them and Kimberly couldn't have been more proud of her team and her best friends. They'd all put in long hours, whether they were decorating or setting up chairs with Robyn or in the kitchen with Gabrielle helping prep the menu. Gabrielle was right about one thing: she had the hardest job, because hers took deliberate precision.

Gabrielle had been working on the wedding cake from the moment she'd left Kimberly's office. Baking the layers was the easy part, but the fondant decoration was quite another. If anyone was up for the challenge, it was Gabby. When Kimberly had called Cole to find out the flavor of cake he'd wanted, he'd deferred to her.

"Whatever you like will be just fine with me," he'd said. "My gal isn't all that particular. All she wants is to marry me."

Kimberly wished she could say the same, but she knew if she ever got married that she would want everything just perfect, so she selected a cake she would want from the three ideas Gabrielle had presented to her. She went with a three-tiered square cake with a lace background and cascading roses.

Robyn had done her part, too. The main lawn and waterfall area had been transformed into a Garden of Eden. White roses and hydrangeas adorned the pillars, and a wedding arch adorned with white roses had been erected and swathed in chiffon to frame the bride and groom during the ceremony. Kimberly was amazed at what Robyn could put together in such a short period of time, and with no help from the groom.

But now that wedding fever was starting to die down and all the elements were in place, Kimberly didn't want to go to the wedding. Her staff was quite capable of handling the event in her absence. How could she stand there and watch Cole pledge his love to some female he'd known for all of two seconds when Jaxon had just walked out of her life? She couldn't do it. It would just be too hard to watch another couple's bliss when her own had been torn away.

Was it terrible of her to leave this on Gabrielle and Robyn's shoulders? Yes. She recognized she was being selfish, but she needed to take this time to grieve for a love that she would never have. Last night she'd been so exhausted from the wedding preparations that she'd come back to her condo and fallen asleep. But her body, her traitorous body, hadn't forgotten what it was like to have Jaxon sleeping beside her. Her body hadn't forgotten the way he'd held her in his arms as they slept or the way it had felt having him drive deep inside her, bringing her the ultimate pleasure.

She needed her friends to take one for the team tonight and let her drown her sorrows in a tub of ice cream.

When Gabby and Robyn arrived on her doorstep wearing matching strapless red chiffon dresses to take her to

Cole's wedding, Kimberly dropped the bomb. "I'm not going."

"Excuse me?" Gabrielle asked.

"I don't understand," Robyn said.

"I can't watch two people vow to love each other for the rest of their days," Kimberly responded. "Not now. It's too much, too soon after Jaxon. I just need some time," she said, walking back into her condo. "Time to get over him."

Gabrielle and Robyn looked each other. "We'll cover for you," the both said nearly in unison.

"I know how hard it is when your heart's been broken," Robyn said. "But you will get through this."

"Until then, we've got your back," Gabrielle replied. "And I'll bring you back a piece of that splendid cake I created."

Kimberly smiled from the couch, where she'd parked herself with her favorite ice cream. "Thanks, girls, it means a lot to me."

Seconds later, they were out the door, leaving Kimberly blessedly alone so she could cry in peace over the wedding she would never have with the man she loved. She reached for the remote and turned on the television.

She was just into her movie when she heard loud pounding on the door of her condo. Who the heck could that be? She'd told the girls she wasn't going and they'd said they would take care of everything. Was there a problem? She rushed to her door and swung it open.

Cole was standing there, holding a garment bag. He was dressed in jeans and a T-shirt, with a big *C* necklace hanging from his neck.

"Cole? What are you doing here?" She glanced down at her watch. The wedding was in an hour. "You should be getting dressed. The photographer will be at your suite any minute."

He pointed at her attire. She was wearing a Belleza cashmere bathrobe, pajamas and her hair was tied up in a scarf as she usually did before she went to bed.

"You need to get dressed," he said, storming into her condo.

"Why?"

"Because I'm not getting married unless you're there to oversee everything."

"You don't need me. Robyn, the Belleza's event manager, has everything under control. You'll be in good hands."

"I don't want Robyn. I want you," Cole stated. "Was Robyn the person I asked to pull off this wedding? No, I called you, because I went to the top. I knew you would ensure the event went off without a hitch."

Kimberly thought about it. He was right. He *had* called her.

"You have twenty minutes to get your act together and get dressed," Cole said, folding his arms across his chest. "Or you risk losing that substantial bonus I agreed to. Here's a dress." He handed her the garment bag. "I'll see you in twenty."

Kimberly's eyes narrowed. Of course he would throw money into the mix. She gave a fake smile. "All right, I'll be there." She pushed him toward the door. "Go get dressed and I'll see you at the lawn."

She saw Cole's triumphant smile as she closed the door. Just great! She had no choice but to put on the dress and attend the wedding.

After a quick shower, Kimberly got ready in record time. When she opened the garment bag, she was amazed at the dress inside. It wasn't any old dress. It was a one-of-a-kind designer gown. The color wasn't white or ivory, but was more like a ginger shade with tons of delicate floral beadwork over sheer lace on the cap-sleeved bodice. It was simply stunning and Kimberly let out a long breath.

Cole was giving her this designer gown to wear to his wedding? Wouldn't she upstage his bride? But if she didn't wear it, would he take offense? She couldn't offend such a high-profile, influential client who could bring back plenty of repeat business, so she put it on.

The dress was made for her body. It fit her every curve and highlighted her slender figure. Kimberly felt like a million bucks in it and it certainly helped lift her spirits. Such an exceptional dress called for great hair, so she swept her hair into a simple updo with a few curls cascading down the back, applied some quick strokes of makeup, her favorite pair of chandelier earrings and silver sandals and headed out the door. She sped in her golf cart toward the main lawn, where the ceremony was being held. She'd taken longer than twenty minutes, but she hoped she wasn't too late.

She parked the golf cart, grabbed the bottom of the dress and took off at a quick pace. That was when she heard the wedding march. When she arrived, she found Robyn and Gabrielle at the entrance to the ceremony, but they were blocking her view of the arch.

"Am I late?" Kimberly glanced at her smiling friends as she smoothed her dress. She hadn't been prepared to come to this event tonight and felt rushed. "I just heard the music."

"No, you're fine," Robyn answered. "Cole told us you were coming, so we held it off until you arrived. The wedding is just starting."

"Thank God!" Kimberly let out a sigh of relief.

"Kim, you look amazing," Gabrielle said.

"Do I really?" Kimberly blushed as she could see Gabrielle tearing up and it was so unlike Gabby. What was going on? "It isn't too much, is it? I mean when I saw this dress, it looked like a wedding gown and I wouldn't want to upstage the bride."

Robyn grinned at her. "Wouldn't be possible."

"Let's get going," Gabrielle said, grasping her hand and giving it a quick squeeze. "We'll go first and then you can follow behind us."

Kimberly nodded. "Okay."

Her friends walked down the aisle but Kimberly hesitated. It was a cruel twist of fate for her to walk down an aisle when she herself might never get the opportunity to do so for real. Would she ever find another man with whom she would share an easy camaraderie and earth-shattering orgasms?

Kimberly breathed in deep, reminding herself that this night wasn't about her, but about Cole and his fiancée. She merely needed to get through the night and then she could go back home, crawl into her bed and cry her eyes out for the love she'd so freely given to Jaxon but that had not been reciprocated.

She turned around and with her head hung low began to follow her friends down the aisle strewn with white rose petals. When she finally glanced up, nothing could have prepared her for the scene in front of her.

Cole was nowhere to be seen. Instead, Jaxon was standing under the arch in a white tuxedo.

Jaxon? She hadn't seen him in over a week and her heart skipped a beat. What was he doing here? She didn't understand. Was he Cole's best man? And why did he have to look so darn good in that tuxedo?

Slowly, she made her way down the aisle and when she made it to the arch, Jaxon was smiling at her.

"What are you doing here?" she whispered.

"I'm sorry for the subterfuge," he replied, "but Cole isn't coming."

"I don't understand." Kimberly stared at Jaxon and then glanced to her left at her friends. That was when she saw the two of them holding bouquets. "What's going on?" she asked them.

Jaxon answered her. "There is no wedding. That is, unless *you* want one."

"Me?" Kimberly stared at him, perplexed, not sure she'd heard right. It didn't make any sense. What did she have to do with any of this?

"I guess my message isn't clear," Jaxon responded. "I was an idiot."

"He's right on that point," she heard one of her friends say behind her.

Kimberly's stomach began to form knots and her heart began palpitating loudly in her chest. What did all of this mean?

Jaxon took her in his. "Kimberly, I'm sorry I left here the way I did. I was confused and scared of my feelings for you."

"You broke my heart," she murmured as a solitary tear escaped down her cheeks.

"I know and I'm sorry." He wiped away her tear with the pad of his thumb. "But I had a lot of things to work out. You see, I never thought real love was possible. And then I met you. And I began to feel emotions I'd never felt before and it scared me."

"Don't you think I was scared, too?" Kimberly said.

"You scared?" Jaxon shook his head. "No, you were fearless. You told me how you felt and that you would accept nothing less. By breaking up with me, you gave me the kick in the butt I needed. While I was away, spending lonely days and nights without you, it made me crazy. It made me realize that I couldn't live without you, Kim."

"You can't?" Could she hope that he had the same feelings for her that she had for him?

He shook his head. "And now I'm ready to tell you without any fears, without any doubts, that I love you, Kimberly Parker."

Kimberly's heart filled with joy.

"And once I knew I loved you, I knew what I had to do." He motioned to the intimate ceremony he'd created. "I reached out to Cole and told him my elaborate plan to win you back and he agreed to help me. Who would have known that's he's a die-hard romantic?"

"A wedding?" Kim sputtered, glancing around her. "Don't you think that's going a bit too far?"

"Maybe," Jaxon conceded, shrugging his shoulders. "But I know in my heart it's where we are going to wind up one day. I understand this may be a bit surreal and if you're not ready yet, I understand. *I* will wait for *you*."

Kimberly couldn't believe her ears. A week ago, Jaxon hadn't been able to bring himself to say the *L* word and now this?

The next thing she knew Jaxon was getting down on one knee. He opened his tuxedo jacket and pulled a ring box out of his pocket.

"Kimberly, I love you. I probably have since the first day I laid eyes on you. And I'm ready to spend the rest of my life proving to you just how much I love you. Will you marry me?"

Kimberly was floored, not just by his words, but by his proposal. She didn't want to waste another minute being away from him and flung herself into his arms. "Yes, yes, yes, I'll marry you. I love you. I love you, Jaxon." She kissed his mouth repeatedly.

"You will?" Jaxon asked, rising to his feet and bringing her with him.

"Yes, I'll marry you, but not today."

"Fair enough." Jaxon beamed, kissing her cheek, her nose and then her forehead. "Just as long as I know that you'll have me for the rest of our days."

"Oh, I'll have you." Kimberly beamed.

From behind them, she heard Gabrielle say, "We now pronounce you fiancé and fiancée."

Kimberly and Jaxon kissed each other with the passion they'd held inside over the past week.

When they separated, they looked at each other for several long moments. "I love you, Jaxon Dunham."

"And I love you, Kimberly Parker."

"I guess this means I'm going to have to throw you a real wedding when the time is right?" Robyn asked, interrupting the happy newly engaged couple.

"And beat this?" Kimberly asked, motioning down to her almost-wedding dress.

"I had some help picking out the dress you're wearing," Jaxon said.

"You did?" Kimberly asked.

Jaxon smiled. "Sure did." He glanced at Robyn and Gabby. "Your friends helped me out."

Kimberly turned to them and her eyes filled with tears. She should have known her best friends had a hand in this.

Robyn gestured to the gown and the surroundings. "If I did all of this in twenty-four hours, imagine what I can do with more time."

"And the cake?" Kimberly turned to Gabrielle with Jaxon's arm still around her. Her friend's eyes were brimming with tears; Kimberly couldn't recall ever seeing Gabby so affected.

"Oh, did you think I pulled out all the stops?" Gabrielle asked. "Oh, no, I always have a few more tricks up my sleeve."

Just then, Cole came out from behind the arch and began serenading them with a love ballad.

"May I have this dance, soon-to-be Mrs. Jaxon Dunham?" Jaxon stepped away from her and held out his hand.

Kimberly happily accepted it. "You can have this dance and every one after that."

Jaxon took her in his arms and together they swayed to the music.

* * * * *

This summer is going to be hot, hot, hot
with a new miniseries
from fan-favorite authors!

YAHRAH ST. JOHN
LISA MARIE PERRY
PAMELA YAYE

HEAT WAVE
OF DESIRE

HOT SUMMER
NIGHTS

HEAT OF
PASSION

Available June 2015

Available July 2015

Available August 2015

California Desert Dreams

HARLEQUIN®
www.Harlequin.com

KPHSNC0615

REQUEST YOUR FREE BOOKS!

2 FREE NOVELS
PLUS 2 FREE GIFTS!

KIMANI™
ROMANCE

Love's ultimate destination!

YES! Please send me 2 FREE Harlequin® Kimani™ Romance novels and my 2 FREE gifts (gifts are worth about $10). After receiving them, if I don't wish to receive any more books, I can return the shipping statement marked "cancel." If I don't cancel, I will receive 4 brand-new novels every month and be billed just $5.44 per book in the U.S. or $5.99 per book in Canada. That's a savings of at least 16% off the cover price. It's quite a bargain! Shipping and handling is just 50¢ per book in the U.S. and 75¢ per book in Canada.* I understand that accepting the 2 free books and gifts places me under no obligation to buy anything. I can always return a shipment and cancel at any time. Even if I never buy another book, the two free books and gifts are mine to keep forever.

168/368 XDN GH4P

Name _____
              (PLEASE PRINT)

Address _____ Apt. #

City _____ State/Prov. _____ Zip/Postal Code

Signature (if under 18, a parent or guardian must sign)

Mail to the **Reader Service:**
IN U.S.A.: P.O. Box 1867, Buffalo, NY 14240-1867
IN CANADA: P.O. Box 609, Fort Erie, Ontario L2A 5X3

Want to try two free books from another line?
Call 1-800-873-8635 or visit www.ReaderService.com.

* Terms and prices subject to change without notice. Prices do not include applicable taxes. Sales tax applicable in N.Y. Canadian residents will be charged applicable taxes. Offer not valid in Quebec. This offer is limited to one order per household. Not valid for current subscribers to Harlequin® Kimani™ Romance books. All orders subject to credit approval. Credit or debit balances in a customer's account(s) may be offset by any other outstanding balance owed by or to the customer. Please allow 4 to 6 weeks for delivery. Offer available while quantities last.

Your Privacy—The Reader Service is committed to protecting your privacy. Our Privacy Policy is available online at www.ReaderService.com or upon request from the Reader Service.

We make a portion of our mailing list available to reputable third parties that offer products we believe may interest you. If you prefer that we not exchange your name with third parties, or if you wish to clarify or modify your communication preferences, please visit us at www.ReaderService.com/consumerschoice or write to us at Reader Service Preference Service, P.O. Box 9062, Buffalo, NY 14240-9062. Include your complete name and address.

He's going beyond
the call of duty…

Stallion
MAGIC

DEBORAH
FLETCHER
MELLO

Noah Stallion never thought he'd reconnect with Catherine Moore—
his childhood crush turned beautiful and savvy businesswoman. Then
their high school reunion provides them with the chance to rekindle
their sizzling attraction. But with an obsessive stalker targeting her,
Catherine is extremely vulnerable. Noah can't let the best thing that
ever happened to both of them get away…no matter the risk.

THE STALLIONS

"Drama, hot sex, attention to detail and a thrilling story line filled with
twists and turns make this book a hard one to put down. A must-read."
—*RT Book Reviews* on *Hearts Afire*

Available June 2015!

www.Harlequin.com

KPDFM4060615

Island heat...

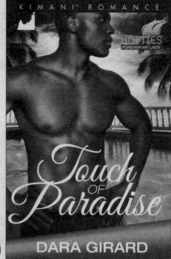

Touch
OF
Paradise

DARA GIRARD

Ten years ago, Aaron Wethers saved Rebecca Cromwell from drowning. Although they went their separate ways, they never forgot each other. Now his Caribbean resort is hosting Rebecca's fashion collection, and she has two weeks to show Aaron how much she's grown up. But when a series of dangerous events threaten to sabotage her show, can he be the hero she needs?

"Romance with a hint of intrigue and mystery makes this novel a must-read and one that readers will never forget."
—*RT Book Reviews* on *A Secret Paradise*

www.Harlequin.com

Available June 2015!

KPDG4070615

His game...
her rules!

The
LOVE
GAME

Regina Hart

Tyler Anderson is poised to take over his family's company. But first he must team up with self-made marketing consultant Iris Beharie. Landing the Anderson Adventures account could save Iris's fledgling PR firm. And as Tyler sheds his introverted image in the bedroom, things heat up in the boardroom. Amid distrust and treachery, is Ty ready to gamble everything on a love that's as real as it gets?

THE ANDERSON FAMILY

Available June 2015!

HARLEQUIN®
www.Harlequin.com

KPRI-H4080615